From Plymouth Notch to President

The Farm Boyhood of Calvin Coolidge

From Plymouth Notch to President

The Farm Boyhood of Calvin Coolidge

KENNETH WEBB

Illustrations by Florence Baker Karpin

The Countryman Press

TAFTSVILLE, VERMONT 05073

ISBN 0-914378-44-9

Printed in the United States of America by Whitman Press, Inc., Lebanon, New Hampshire

CONTENTS

	Foreword	vii
I	THE "LONER"	1
II	GALUSHA COOLIDGE	7
III	PRACTICAL JOKES CAN BE INHERITED!	13
IV	"THE LORD TAKETH AWAY"	18
V	MUSIC IN THE MOUNTAINS	27
VI	LOST IN THE WILDERNESS	35
VII	"GO UP HIGHER"	48
VIII	BLACK RIVER ACADEMY	58
IX	SPRINGTIME TO HARVEST	68
X	COUNTRY SQUIRE	73
XI	PEGASUS TAKES OFF.	80
XII	FORMULA FOR GREATNESS	91
	Epilog	99

FOREWORD

This is not primarily a juvenile, though many perceptive teen-agers will enjoy it. *Plymouth Notch to President* is really a picture of a mountain village and its rugged, honest, kindly people; it is a study of how this environment shaped the life and destiny of an intelligent, sensitive boy.

Calvin Coolidge made it plain that he didn't regard himself as a genius, or even as especially talented. But the rugged mountains in which he grew up, the severe climate, and particularly the plain, hard-working people, his forebears and his neighbors, molded his character, giving him the determination, the attention to detail, the unsparing effort which enabled him by successive small steps to climb to the pre-eminence he himself was surprised to find himself achieving. As he wrote many years later, "Persistence and determination alone are omnipotent."

It makes a good story — inspiring, entertaining, stimulating. I hope readers will enjoy it as much as I have enjoyed digging out the facts on which the story is based. A piece of fictionalized biography like this doesn't pretend to be an historical account of actual conversations and incidents. But I have tried to know the principal character and the supporting cast well enough to have a feel for what was in character and what was not.

For instance, in the first chapter I wanted to use the old couplet about the load of hay in June. I had Mrs. Coolidge, Calvin's mother, quoting that; but that didn't seem quite in character for her: she was a village girl, and an adage referring to haying wouldn't suggest itself to her so readily as to some country girl who would know the value of early hay. This led me to try to find out who the girl was who kept house for Mrs. Coolidge in her last illness. It was a rewarding search, for it led me to Beth Smith — Mrs. Earl (Round) Smith — and her brother, George Round, both of Rutland. Beth and George Round were the children of Stella (McWain) Round. Stella was the younger sister of Martha McWain, later Mrs. John Wilder, the country girl who was housekeeper for Mrs. Coolidge in her last year. Beth Smith has helped me with many types of material, both oral and written, notably the reminiscences of Charles Scott of Tyson. The incident of Letty's hat is based on a story Mrs. Smith had written.

It was Sally Thompson, secretary to the Coolidge Foundation, author of *Growing Up In Plymouth Notch, 1872-1895*, who gave me the addresses of these descendants of Stella McWain. Sally Thompson also pointed out that Calvin and his friend Dell Ward would never have camped out over night at Nineveh. This led, through some information from Mrs. Allen Fletcher (Zoa Townsend) of Ludlow, to the episode of the two boys getting themselves lost in the Nineveh wilderness.

The director of the Black River Academy Historical Museum, Milton Moore of Ludlow and Plymouth, has been the source of much information about the old Academy. It was he who gave me the compendious publication on the Academy published in 1972.

Kate Ward, the widow of Oric Ward, who was Dell Ward's brother, is a lady now over ninety. She has been the source of many tidbits of early history. Her daughter, Lisa Hoskison, and Charles Hoskison, Kate Ward's son-in-law, have been helpful with corroborative details.

Earl Brown of Plymouth has also pointed out a couple of changes which were made. All in all, the manuscript has had the thoughtful concern of a number of good friends. Errors may well remain, but they should be minor.

Of printed sources, the *Autobiography*, of course, has been a main-stay. It is frustrating sometimes in the detail it leaves *out*, as for instance, the name of the remarkable blacksmith who stood at John Coolidge's forge. Merrill was one of these blacksmiths, but I have not been able to get any sure indication that that was the fine blacksmith of whom Coolidge writes with such appreciation. Why didn't he just give the man's *name!*

Blanche Brown Bryant's monumental work entitled *Genealogical Records of the Founders and Early Settlers of Plymouth, Vermont* has been of inestimable help in keeping the generations straight, and in working out a number of puzzling questions of the inter-relations through marriage of various families.

Besides the publication of the Black River Academy Museum, mentioned above, a whole book on the events in Bennington on the 19th of August, 1891, came into my hands through the aid of Weston Cate, Jr., director of the Vermont Historical Society. The book was a gold mine, doubly appreciated because very few people, apparently, even know of its existence.

The little book by Ernest Carpenter titled *The Boyhood Days of President Calvin Coolidge* has been helpful in pointing up special events at Plymouth, and old-time institutions like the Singing Class.

The *Memoirs* of Charles Scott, son of Dr. Scott, a local physician in Coolidge's day, gave me the bantie egg story (only in Scott it was a quid of chewing tobacco, dropped by a young farm hand).

A publication of the Forbes Library in Northhampton contributed the chronological summary. *Your Son Calvin*, and *Meet Calvin Coolidge*, both edited by Edward Lathem of the Baker Library in Hanover, have been helpful with background, as have other books relating to Coolidge though not dealing with his early years.

In contributing data, publications, and commentary during the writing of *Plymouth Notch To President*, John and Florence Coolidge have been of continuing assistance.

To all these good people and rich sources, I acknowledge my indebtedness with sincere thanks.

Kenneth B. Webb
March 1978

I

THE "LONER"

In the early morning of a promising June day, the sun was just climbing over the Plymouth hills. A slender, wiry youngster of eleven, with reddish hair and freckled face, sat dangling his bare feet over the edge of a farmhouse stoop, watching the sun gild first one, then another of the knolls in a rolling pasture. Dressed in shirt and overalls, the boy was absorbed in this miracle of returning day when the stocky figure of another lad about his own age appeared around the corner of the house.

"Whatcha doin', Cal?" the visitor asked.

"Nothing."

"Whatcha thinkin', then."

"Spotty could of dropped her calf."

"Yeah, she's about due, ain't she?"

"Last night, Pa says, or tonight. Wanna go see? She got away from the rest when they came in for milking. We couldn't find her later on." Young Calvin Coolidge slid down from the stoop and headed toward the pasture, knowing that his chum, Dell Ward, would want to share this adventure, as he had so many others. "Pa says when you're looking for a new calf in a pasture you hafta *be* the cow and figure where you'd have your calf. Away from enemies. Behind some bushes maybe."

"They's lotsa bushes up in that corner by the granite outcrop,"

Dell offered, pointing to a far stretch of pasture. "Where we got that old woodchuck last year — remember?" Dell realized that his friend was not following him. Cal had stopped, and was eyeing a ravine. "If *I* was a cow," Cal mused, "I'd head for a place like that. Kind of hard to get to, and that's *good.*"

The boys picked their way cautiously down the steep slope of the little valley. They searched the area on the down side of the ravine till it flattened out into meadowland. Retracing their steps, and avoiding almost by instinct the thistles that grew in untroubled profusion in this forgotten area, they made their way upward till the occasional bushes became denser. No sign of Spotty.

"Too much brush here," Cal remarked. "No place to lie down."

"They's lotsa good places in that corner I told you about."

"Come on." Cal started for the far corner at a speed that made his friend stretch to keep up with him.

"Godfrey, Cal, Spotty ain't gonna run away. What's the hurry?"

"Want to get there."

The boys beat their way back and forth through the brushy corner. Still no sign of Spotty.

"She ain't here, Cal."

Cal appeared not to notice this statement of the obvious. His chum was used to these silences.

"You know," Cal said at last, "if I was Spotty and I wanted to hide, I'd pick a ravine like the one we searched, but with a brook or a spring. There's one like that up by the other corner."

"You figure a cow can think that much?"

Cal was already off with his eager stride to the other corner. "Instinct," he remarked. "Pa told me a lot about instinct when we drove over the Pass to the Rutland Fair. Pa knows animals."

The boys approached the lower reaches of another ravine, smaller, cut out of the slope of an upland shoulder. A runnel of clear water wound its way through grassy sedge and was lost in the deep herbage below.

"She's here," Cal announced confidently, stopping to roll up his pants legs.

"How do you know?"

"Hoof prints — fresh."

Dell stopped to study the prints. "Hmmm," he observed, bending over for a closer look, "Don't have to be Spot's."

Cal was already out of sight, wading up the little brook. In his haste to catch up, Dell got the bottoms of his overalls covered with mud.

"Found her," the voice floated down to Dell from some distance ahead. "Heifer."

Parting the final clump of alders, Dell came out to a grassy spot where Spot was lying at ease, licking a little black and white calf. "She's a beaut, ain't she?" Dell remarked.

"She's perfect. Come on. I want to tell Pa — and Mama." Cal quickened his pace as he approached the old homestead. "Pa's going to be tickled when he knows she's a heifer."

When the boys reached the porch, the kitchen door opened, and a tall man in his early forties stepped out on the stoop. "Calvin, you're late for break — You found her? So Spotty *did* calve. Bull or heifer?"

"Heifer. Black and white."

"She's a beaut," Dell added.

"Well, Spotty, congratulations," Calvin's father said, as if the cow were there. "You did well by us. Mother'll be glad to know it's a heifer again," he added, with a pleased glance at his son. "Dell, have you had breakfast? Come in anyway and sit with us. P'raps you could eat a flapjack? Hot with maple syrup? Sure you can."

Four people sat around the breakfast table in the kitchen: John Coolidge, whose tall, spare form seemed to reach the low ceiling; Cal's eight-year-old sister Abbie, and Mrs. Coolidge, half reclining in an arm chair close to the table. A young "girl," Martha McWain, who was housekeeper for Mrs. Coolidge, made the fourth.

"Dell, can't you manage a pancake or two?" Mrs. Coolidge asked. "New run maple syrup. It's good."

"Ours is great this year, too," Dell said as he drew up a chair. "Uncle Jim says it's one of the best sugarin' years he's seen. We're hayin' today, and I came over to see if Cal could help me turn hay. We got a lot down yistidy."

Mr. Coolidge cleared his throat. "That's fine, Dell, and I wish Calvin could work with you. But I knocked down some hay yesterday too, and we plan to get it in this morning when the dew's off, then turn the hay in the swale and get that in afterwards. Sorry, Calvin," John added, noting his son's disappointment.

"Everyone's getting in hay early this year," Martha observed.

> "Load of hay in June's worth a silver spoon; Load of hay in July isn't worth a fly," Martha McWain quoted.

"If I help Dell, then he can come and help us." Cal suggested.

"No, both hay fields need laborers, both for the turning, soon's the dew's off, and for the loading. Tell you what," Mr. Coolidge added, seeing both boys' disappointment, "If both of you help with your own haying till dinner time, then if Dell's folks are willing, you could both take a quick trip down to Woodward's Pond for a little fishing, so long, Calvin, as you promise to be back in time for a load of the swale hay before chores and supper. Think your folks will agree to that, Dell?" The Coolidge smile was disarming.

* * *

"Let's fish from that old raft that's tied up down by Bishops'," Dell suggested, as the pair set out past the Hall place and down the Notch road — the old stage-coach road — to the Woodward Reservoir, still known as Woodward's Pond. "Raft's a good place for the big ones, down underneath."

Dell's guess about the "big ones" proved good. Not long after the pair had put their lines in — Dell by the outer corner of the log raft, his companion near him on the opposite outer corner — Dell shouted, "I got a big one." With that, Dell made a sudden lunge which backed him into his chum.

Cal heard the shout, clutched vainly at the air to catch his balance, teetered on the edge of the raft, then saw the water suddenly rushing up to meet him. As he hit the surface he closed his eyes tight. He remembered wondering if he would drown. Swimming wasn't his specialty, though his father had taught him to keep afloat, and to do the "dog-paddle."

The boy's feet touched bottom, and he waded rather than swam ashore. But he had been badly frightened. Many farm boys couldn't swim at all, and Cal had no illusions about really keeping himself afloat. He headed straight up the bank, his clothes dripping. "Bring the poles," he called back to Dell. "The water's cold as ice."

That evening at the supper table there were "words" between Cal's father and his mother. It was as near to serious disagreement as the pair had come since Mrs. Coolidge got the "wasting disease," consumption. "You aren't going to let Calvin go down to that pond all by himself, are you?" Mrs. Coolidge asked. "He can't practice his swimming all alone, can he?"

"Yes, my love, I think he'll have to. I can't always go down with him, what with all I have to do. Cal's got a natural caution. And he's a loner. That's both bad and good. As he gets older, it may cheat him out of some good times; but it also gives him the chance to think things out, weigh them and ponder them and understand them. He's got the knowledge now of how to take care of himself in the water. I know it sounds bad. But all he needs is practice."

"But do let's insist that Dell or somebody go with him," Mrs. Coolidge pleaded.

"Dell can't swim," Cal remarked.

II

GALUSHA COOLIDGE

People are different. They're interested in different things, or in different ways of looking at the same thing.

This important discovery twelve-year-old Cal had just made. He was sitting on the top step of the back porch of his grandfather's farm house little more than a stone's throw from his own home in the village. He was gazing at his grandfather's big barn, now his father's. The boy was pondering the way his father had just spoken of Spotty's little heifer, brought into the barn to be weaned.

"We'll have to remember to speak to Merrill about dehorning her," his father had remarked.

"Grandpa didn't do that to Spotty when she was little," Cal had objected.

"Well, your grandfather was different. He didn't realize how much better folks now-a-days like a cow you don't have to watch for fear she'll swing her head around suddenly to get rid of a fly."

Cal remembered now that this same matter had come up when Spotty herself was little some five or six years before. When John Coolidge had asked Cal's grandfather how long before the heifer would be de-horned, his grandfather had reached down and patted the little animal. "A cow doesn't like to have her horns cut off," he had replied slowly. "Makes her feel she's not quite all a cow. Like a woman's hair. Besides, a cow looks better with her horns. See that nice curve on her mother's horns? And the glossy sheen of light and dark on them?"

Cal remembered how his grandfather had gazed down at the little beast with a look in his eye the boy didn't then understand. Now all of a sudden he did. Grandfather Coolidge loved the heifer. He loved all his animals the same way: his horses, his cows, his sheep, even his chickens, those with the beautiful black and white feathers. He felt the same way about his cannas and his dahlias, prizing them for their beauty.

Cal's father was more likely to look at the value of a thing in money. He was a sharp trader. He was proud, for instance, of having bought their present house for $300, getting back immediately $100 from selling off an unwanted barn. Cal could see both sides, both ways of looking at things.

Galusha Coolidge was an ideal grandfather. Although he had died when Cal was only six, much of the old man was built into his grandson. Cal's mind flashed back to those earlier years. Grandpa Coolidge was never too busy to stop what he was doing and greet his little grandchildren. When Cal was six and Abbie only three, Cal would take his sister by the hand and walk over to see Grandma and Grandpa Coolidge. If it was chore time, the pair would spot the tall, spare form of their grandfather moving about the barnyard.

"See my early dahlias?" he would ask. "Aren't they pretty, Abbie? Ever see anything redder than they are, or bigger? They're choice stock. Peter Henderson's best. And let me show you something." Grandpa ducked into the grain room of the old barn and brought out a small measure of corn. The nondescript barnyard fowl would gather round, but also a striking cluster of very large fowl would appear with feathered legs, their black tails and neck feathers contrasting with their pure white bodies.

"Aren't they beautiful?" their grandfather would ask, with almost a note of reverence in his voice. "These are some of the best Light Brahmas in Vermont. Just traded a dozen hens for this pen. Oh, they're tame, Abbie. They won't hurt you. And the geese are gone. How many are there, Calvin?"

One, two, three, four — four hens and a rooster. That's five."

"Right. They're young stock, so they're four pullets and a cockerel. That makes what they call a 'pen.' Breeding stock. Think how beautiful a whole barnyard full of these birds will be. Look at the nice feathers on their legs, Abbie."

"Where's the peacocks?" the little girl asked.

"The peacocks? Two of the peahens have stolen nests and are planning to raise families. Hear that? One of the peacocks just made that churring call again. They're down in the meadow. Don't run. Farm children never run when there's stock around. And don't get too near them. The peacocks don't like folks coming around their hens when they're setting. See these tall nasturtiums, Abbie. They're going to climb way up this brush around the kitchen door. See how gay these first blossoms are. Deep orange, almost scarlet."

"Does the buff Cochin rooster think he can lick the big Brahma?" Cal asked. "Look, he's going right up to the Brahma."

"Oh, the Brahma won't pay any attention. Look, when he stands tall he's amost as tall as Abbie. That little Cochin and his wife got through the brush around their yard. And here's the other Cochin hen, with her new family of chicks. Let's see if we can find where they got out."

The three started for the little coop beside the barn where the Cochins were kept. Grandpa Coolidge's eyes narrowed as he looked out over the meadow where the two peacocks were setting up an alarm. "Isn't that a beautiful meadow, Calvin? Remember, there's no way of life better than being a farmer. He's richer every fall than he was the year before. It's hard work, but it's a good life. Look at what we have here. By God's grace we've been able to increase and multiply his generous bounty. I may not be around always, Calvin, so remember what I say. There's no better way to live than on a farm. In fact, it's the only right way to live. You see God's wonders everywhere."

Grandpa was like that. Religious. And he lived his religion. Nobody could be more generous or more kindly. Like the time when Grandpa had taken small Calvin with him on a trip down Tyson way with his team.

Grandpa had been sorry for a man down at Tyson, a loud and

profane teamster who lived by picking up odd jobs for his fine team of chestnut bays. Unfortunately, Joe Jessup's voice was as loud as it was profane. Neighbors for a mile around were treated to exact information on the various kinds of perdition to which his horses were consigned. Joe meant nothing by this, and the horses got used to it, taking it all in stride, like the equally stentorian directions as to when to "gee" and when to "haw." Joe loved his horses, and was proud of their strength.

On the way to Tyson Grandpa Coolidge had met up with Joe, compared their respective teams, and Joe had remarked that he hadn't yet got in his winter supply of wood.

"You free tomorrow, Joe?" Mr. Coolidge asked.

"Yup, free every day."

"Then come up with me after morning chores and we'll both go get a load of limb wood from the Lime Kiln Lot. When I got out my logs last year for the barn addition, I left the tops and the limb-wood. They're dry now, dry hard wood. You can have as much as you can haul. Won't cost you anything but the hauling. I want to get those tops out of there so I can turn it back to forest."

The trip to get limb-wood was one of Cal's favorite memories of his grandfather. He was riding on the wagon seat beside him with Joe Jessup's team close behind. They came to a point where the road divided. Grandpa got down from his seat and strode back to where Joe had stopped his team. "Joe, this road to the right gets to the cut-over parcel in the Lime Kiln Lot quicker'n the one I have to take with my team. There's a mud hole down that way, but with a young team like yours, and strong as they are, you'll have no trouble with the mud hole."

"I might as well stick along with you."

"Your team can't pull through the mud hole? Not strong enough?"

"Strong? Sure they're strong. Just for that, I'll take the lower road."

"Well, see you at the Lime Kiln not, Joe. You'll get there before I do. Use your ax on any tops you see handy by."

As they drove along, Grandpa got very quiet. When Cal kept on asking questions, Grandpa laid his hand on the boy's shoulder.

"Hear that flicker? Corn planting time when the flicker calls. Listen . . ."

Cal missed the flicker, but suddenly the loudest string of oaths the boy had ever heard floated up from the direction Mr. Jessup had taken.

"Must have got into that bees' nest beside the mud hole," Grandpa chuckled.

In fact, Grandpa kept chuckling off and on for the rest of the trip to the Lime Kiln Lot. Now Calvin could see why. Grandpa knew about the bees, but Joe Jessup wouldn't figure he hadn't taken the lower road of his own free will.

Grandpa Coolidge took to his bed soon after this. He loved to have six-year old Calvin read to him from the Gospel of John. "In the beginning was the Word, and the Word was with God, and the Word was God." The meaning here was beyond the boy, but the words he could mostly read, though haltingly. Some of the words, like "comprehended," were beyond him, but anything from the Gospels was familiar territory and Grandpa loved it.

"When I was your age, or perhaps a little mite older, this is the way I used to read to *my* grandfather in *his* last illness . . ."

"Last illness?" Cal pondered the words as he came out of the bedroom. Finding his grandmother in the kitchen, he went up to her. "Is — is Grandpa going to die, Grandma?"

"Well, we hope not. But you know, 'The Lord giveth, and the Lord taketh away.'"

A few weeks later a very sober Calvin followed his father and mother, sister Abbie, his grandmother, and all the Coolidge relatives and friends to the little cemetery on the hillside south of the Village. His grandfather had been much beloved by everyone, and there was a large crowd for the funeral not only from the other hamlets in Plymouth township, Five Corners, The Notch, The Union, Frog City, The Kingdom, Tyson and Nineveh, but from far beyond. But why was it that the Lord taketh away? Grandpa wasn't really old. Calvin had his "cry"; now he could contemplate this change called death in a mood which was sad, but not despairing.

III

PRACTICAL JOKES CAN BE INHERITED

The little white church at the Notch was so small that it had only a simple balcony running straight across above the vestibule. Five chairs on either side of the main floor flanked the central door from the vestibule into the church itself. These two sets of chairs accommodated an overflow at Christmas and Easter. Some of the "regulars" preferred these hard chairs to the harder pews. One of the regulars, "Old Vizly," had brought in a comfortable chair of his own, and generally dozed off during the ninety-minute sermon. Although he served as the able moderator of the annual town meeting, Old Vizly had almost no formal education. In reading the articles on which the town meeting was to vote, he always pronounced as "vizly" the old term "viz." — namely — perhaps on the analogy with "secondly" or "thirdly." As this gentleman relaxed and then drifted off to sleep when the parson was well launched on his sermon, Old Vizly's shiny bald head scarcely a dozen feet below the balcony rail made a tempting target for a trio of twelve-year-olds allowed to sit in this gallery — during good behavior.

"How 'bout a hunk of pitch pine gum for that bald pate," Clarence Blanchard asked one Sunday after church let out.

"Aw, it would just roll off," Dell Ward remarked. "How could we get it to stick? That would be funnier."

"Hmmm", from Cal. "What we need is something real sticky.

Kind of runny, too."

"Well, what?" Del Ward challenged his chum.

"I'll study at it a while," Cal promised.

* * *

"Calvin was a good boy — not the best scholar in the class, but among the first half dozen in a group of 30. He was methodical, faithful, honest, punctual." This was the estimate of Ernest Carpenter, his teacher in the old stone schoolhouse beside the cheese factory in the Notch. The boy liked geography, which came in the largest sized text book to accommodate the maps. This extra size accommodated other operations, too, besides studying maps. Long before duplicating machines, a teacher had to write down on the blackboard much of what he or she wanted the students to learn.

Thus it happened that while Mr. Carpenter was writing on the blackboard, there would be a sudden splat, and a soggy over-sized spit-ball would land on the blackboard beside him. No matter how swiftly he turned around, everybody would be hard at work. Not a smile; not a furtive glance. After a frustrated check among suspects, Mr. Carpenter would turn back to his work, only to have another and perhaps soggier missile land beside him.

Ernest Carpenter knew children well enough not to make a big fuss over this. Sometime he would catch the culprit. But according to one authority in town he never succeeded. He never even suspected the quiet boy with the innocent face — and the big geography book.

"By Godfrey, Calvin, you done it again," Clarence Blanchard remarked as the trio wended its way home after one of these episodes.

"Hey, Cal," Dell Ward put in, "how about one of them big ones for old Vizly?"

"Mount do," Cal replied, "but we can do better. Let me study at it some more."

Grandma Coolidge still kept up the old farm much as it was when her husband was there. There were the same noisy geese, the quarrelsome peacocks, the beautiful big Brahmas, the quacking ducks — and the same beautiful red flowers: dahlias, cannas, climbing nasturtiums and zinnias. Calvin found time almost every day to get over to see his grandmother, who taught the little Sunday school in the Notch and had an instinctive, and loving, understanding of children.

One day when Calvin showed up, his grandmother gave him a small brown egg. "Know what this is, Calvin?"

The boy inspected it gravely. "Bantie egg, isn't it?" he asked.

"Right. Remember that old Cochin hen that stole her nest last fall and hatched out a family just as snow came on? She should have had more sense. If they don't get an early start, those Cochin pullets never lay till the next summer. Well, this is the first egg of a first pullet from another family. Take it home and show it to your mother."

But Calvin had additional plans for that egg. "Something sticky and runny — and soft."

Sunday morning came. The little trio of boys gathered by habit on the grass beyond the end of the stone steps to the church vestibule.

"I got the perfect thing for Old Vizly," Calvin said. "This here bantie egg. One of you take it and crack a bit along the middle, then reach out suddenly and open it up. The yolk should fall right splat on Vizly's bald top. The two of you scrunch down together and nobody'll notice you. Parson Meeker can't see that far. I'll sit down at one end of the chairs and tell you what happens. Should be good."

It was a long sermon. Parson Meeker had finally got to "fourthly" or "fifthly" when it happened. Nobody noticed the two hands extended out about a foot from the gallery, or the little egg when it fell, but the reaction was instantaneous.

Old Vizly practically leapt from his chair with an oath. He put his hand up to his head and brought it down covered with something yellow and slimy. He looked at his hand for a moment, then let out a volume of oaths "that never had ought to of been said in a church."

Parson Meeker stopped in the middle of a sentence. Not being a quick thinker in a crisis, he could only speak to the back of Vizly as the man disappeared through the doorway to the vestibule, seeking

privacy: "Ask God's forgiveness for those words," he called out. "Now as I was saying . . . what was I saying?"

There was an agonized pause. Then the parson said, "Let's all stand and sing Hymn number 420."

Calvin noticed his father get up, take a handkerchief from his pocket, and slip out to the vestibule.

At supper when they were reviewing this diverting episode in the church, Calvin's father looked at his son quizzically. "How did it happen, Calvin, that you weren't sitting upstairs there with Clarence and Dell, or downstairs with me, as I'd like you should."

"Oh, various things," Cal replied. "I like to see the people coming in, the ones that come late and such like."

The elder Coolidge opened his mouth to ask a further question, then looked in the direction of his wife, and thought better of it.

Perhaps his wife's family, the Moors, were not such lovers of practical jokes as were the Coolidges.

IV

"THE LORD TAKETH AWAY"

Whenever John Coolidge had to attend a session of the Windsor County Court at Woodstock, the county seat, he took young Calvin along if the trip didn't require taking the boy out of school. Such a trip was always pleasant. The mare knew the way: the elder Coolidge could relax and get to know his shy young son on a deeper level than is possible for many fathers. And going to Woodstock was always a change from a day at the farm, pitching hay or hoeing corn or even digging potatoes with Merrill, the blacksmith who doubled as hired man. Merrill was as excited as Calvin when either of them opened a hill with an unusual number of big, golden nuggets.

The fall session of the Court started before school began. John Coolidge, it seemed to his son, knew 'most everybody in Woodstock. The shire town was to the village boy's eyes a veritable metropolis, with a lively business section and many stately mansions on Elm Street and around The Green.

Several people who knew the Coolidge family inquired after Calvin's mother. "How's Vikki?" they would ask, or "How's Mrs. Coolidge?"

To all these concerned inquiries Mr. Coolidge gave about the same answer: "Well, rather poorly today, I'm sorry to say."

"She doesn't get any better?"

"It's up and down, but the good days are less frequent."

"Oh, I'm so sorry to hear that, John," one elderly lady replied, laying her hand on his father's arm. "Poor Vikki. If there's anything we can do . . ." The speaker looked at young Calvin and left her sentence unfinished. "Well, I'm sure this bracing fall weather will help her to mend," she added.

But both John Coolidge and his elderly friend knew that for tuberculosis there was no cure. Young Calvin had heard enough to strengthen his own fears. His mother's long silences, when he sat beside her at the doorway so Mrs. Coolidge could get the fresh air on a good day, the sadness in her voice sometimes when she finally spoke, troubled him, young as he was.

"Father, is Mother real sick?" the boy asked as they left the village by the old covered bridge at the west end of town.

"Yes, Calvin, I'm afraid she is quite sick. We must face it."

"Will she — will she get better?"

"We pray that she may, son — but whatever happens, I'll try to be both father and —" He stopped suddenly and looked straight ahead.

As the full impact of the situation struck Calvin for the first time, it was more than he could bear. He bent over and his shoulders shook with silent sobs.

His father, now in control of his own emotions, put his arm around the boy's shoulder, and spoke in a low voice. "Look, son, for Mother's sake we'll have to be brave — and cheerful. You musn't let Mother see how you feel. Promise?"

Calvin raised his tear-stained face to look at his father. He even tried to smile. "Yes, Papa," he managed. "I'll try, I'll —" His voice broke.

* * *

The maple leaves had turned scarlet and then drifted to the ground. The oaks were deep bronze. Birch and beech stood stark and gray in the November woods. The orange and yellow calendulas in Grandmother Coolidge's border by the doorway had finally succumbed to the killing frosts.

It was plain also that Vikki Coolidge was slipping away. Calvin sat beside his mother's bed, trying to get all he could of her before she left. After school he and his sister Abbie sat in her bedroom till Calvin had to leave for chores at the barn and Abbie would go to help Martha get supper.

Sometimes Father Coolidge would come to the door of the bedroom and say, "Calvin, Dell and Clarence are waiting for you in the kitchen. They want you should come out for a game of prisoners' base. It's 'most time for chores anyway, and I'll do your milking for you. Come on now — good for you to get out."

The neighbors were as concerned as was John Coolidge to keep up a smooth-running household. Often some village family invited

Calvin and Abbie to supper. Wanting to do something for the Coolidges, others brought in hot dishes, though they knew that Martha McWain was an excellent cook.

Autumn deepened into winter, a mountain winter of merciless, unremitting cold and deep snow. His mother was never far from Calvin's thoughts. He stole quietly about the house; when he went to a neighbor's, he opened the woodshed door quietly and knocked timidly on the kitchen door. Or, as once, he found the kitchen door partly open and overheard the end of a conversation: "When Galusha Coolidge died, that was in December, mid-December. The snow came afore the deep cold, and the ground was hardly froze. But this year the ground's froze real hard, and here it's only January. Vikki can't last till spring; she —"

"Just a minute, Hiram — that you, Calvin? Come in, my boy."

But Vikki lasted till maple sugaring, although the snow still lay deep in the valleys and the ground was frozen. One night in late March John Coolidge came into his son's room. "Your mother is going," he said in a steady voice. "I've got Abbie started. Mother wants to see you both before she leaves. Hurry now, and remember, no crying. Not now. You're almost a man. You'll be doing some of the plowing this spring. I promised you."

Their mother was very weak. She raised her wasted arm with effort, and when she spoke, it was so softly that both children, kneeling by her bed, had to strain to hear her. "Dear Calvin, and little Abbie, you've both been so good to me. Don't grieve too much. I want you to run and play and laugh and sing. Help your dear father as you always have. God bless you, my children. Don't cry. Remember I'm going where the meadows are always green and the sun always shines and —" She stopped, exhausted. "So tired, John, so . . ."

Her husband leaned over the pillow to kiss her. She was gone.

Abbie burst into tears. Calvin's body shook with sobs.

"Have a good cry now, children," their father said gently, touching each of them on the shoulder. "Then we'll get ourselves together. Martha, it's over," he said as he became aware of Martha McWain standing in the doorway, with a handkerchief to her face.

"Do you think you could get dressed and run over to tell Grandma?"

For the next few days, though he had tried to prepare himself for this, Calvin was too numb with grief and the sense of loss to show much emotion. He did his chores — thank God for chores — and he tried to be especially thoughtful of Abbie. The children, always close, supported each other.

"See that Spotty has plenty of hay," his father said, "and some nice corn fodder. You know she's not far from calving. How is Gorgeous George doing? And how did he like the hot mash Martha sent him and his hens this morning?"

Cal smiled faintly. "He liked it," he said. Gorgeous George was the big Brahma rooster Grandfather Galusha Coolidge had bought just before he died. George was still going strong.

"Tell George they'll all be out on grass before too long now," his father went on. "The hens all laying by now?"

Calvin nodded. "Ten eggs yistidy."

"Yesterday," his father corrected him. "Grandma says you may have the money from any eggs you can sell."

* * *

The commital service, when the ground was thawed enough to dig the grave, brought back the keen edge of the boy's grief. But there was in this new grief a philosophical turn his father recognized as part of the approaching maturity of a sensitive, intelligent youngster who had faced a deep sorrow most boys of his age are spared.

On the way home from Woodstock the next time Court held, Cal asked his father, "Why does Grandma say 'The Lord giveth and the Lord taketh away'? Why should He take Mother away when she was so young? She — it was on her thirty-ninth birthday you told that old gentleman in Woodstock. Why should He take her away like that, when we all loved her so, and need her so?"

John Coolidge laid his hand on his son's knee. "Son, I don't hold so much with that quotation. I'm sure the Lord gives us all our blessings; but why a loving Father would do something that seems so cruel, this is hard to understand. Not everything about the Lord is clear to our limited thinking. He's infinite — without limit — and we are limited in our understanding."

"Grandpa Coolidge wasn't old either — only sixty-three. And he loved being alive, and we all loved him. Do you think the Lord is really 'loving'? A boy down at the Union says his pa says there prob'ly isn't any God."

There was a moment of shocked silence, Cal's at having voiced such an idea, his father's at finding his son's faith so shaken. The mare trotted along, following the road she knew so well, the one beside the Ottauquechee.

"Some folks would say the Lord tries people he loves specially, gives them burdens hard to bear. I don't go for that idea either. It's something I feel is natural at times, to wonder, I mean, about God. There's so much about Him we can't understand. But to doubt that there is a God — that's like the fool saying there's no such thing as intelligence."

"I think it was kind of awful for Mother to be kept — kept in that box till the ground thawed."

"Remember, Calvin, Mother wasn't there. She's gone on to — she was sure — a life so wonderful we can't even picture it. Remember the green fields she spoke of, and remember how she loved the sunrise? She'd *left* her body. It's just like the cocoon I showed you hanging to that beam in the barn. By now that cocoon is just a hollow shell — and the little animal in it has flown away as a beautiful butterfly. What could be more wonderful than that?"

"I wonder if anybody ever told that boy down at the Union these things, and what Mother used to say about God?"

"Don't give the boy another thought. I look at it this way. Without God, without some great and loving Creator to put all this together, to bring about the wonders of new life everywhere in the fields, without some Force that could create human personality as wonderful as Mother, some truly loving Spirit as we see it in fine people like the Coolidge and the Moor grandparents, without some great Cause, how could it all happen? On every side we see order — the way the stars sweep the sky and return each night; the way the habit of growth of a whole plant is packed into a tiny seed, the way wonderful, unselfish people show love in their lives. We can't but look at all this with awe. Could it all happen without some master plan? Order, creativity, love — God shows himself in everything we see. Just because we don't see His whole plan, can we doubt that He exists, and is managing things every minute?"

It was a long speech for a Coolidge, usually so sparing of words.

"It's kind of complicated," Cal said.

"Many very smart people have struggled with these problems before us. All we can be sure of — and this we can see all around us — all we can really know is that there must be some great, loving, creative power that manages all these things. It's probably as much beyond us as we are beyond Dolly's understanding. All she knows is that when she brings us home we unhitch her and give her good grain to eat, and a nice warm stall in the winter. But we're different from Dolly, in that we can keep trying to understand more of this Power — and the more we see and begin to understand, the more wonderful it becomes."

They drove on in silence.

Just as they rounded the last turn and came in sight of the cluster of buildings which was Plymouth Notch, Cal turned to his father: "Thank you, Papa. I guess that boy in the Union's kind of dumb."

"Between you and me, I think he is. But we won't tell him so. Everybody has a right to his own views. You get the groceries out of the buggy, then unhitch Dolly and give her her supper. I've got to stop in the store a minute."

* * *

This honest talk with his father had a lasting effect on Calvin. The next spring as he rode Captain, his Grandfather's favorite riding horse, he thought over some of the things they had discussed. The country lanes were turning green with the warm April sun. His favorite ride took him along the little road past the cemetery where his mother's body was buried, the spot he visited so often at dusk after supper and the evening chores were over. Captain liked this road: he went as far as the left turn and the steep hill.

"Captain enjoy the ride?" John Coolidge smiled up at his son as Cal brought the horse to a stop in Grandpa Coolidge's barnyard.

"He didn't say."

"Who was it used to ride the winged horse named Pegasus?" his father asked.

"Bellerophon."

"Good memory of my reading aloud to you. Put Captain out to pasture again and come sit with me in the carriage shed here. There's something I want to talk with you about."

"You're right that Captain needs more riding," Cal remarked as he rounded the corner of the shed. Soon's I took the bit out of his mouth he kicked up his heels and set out at full gallop over the hill. I haven't let him out like that since — since last year."

"You'll get back to it, feeling the wind through your hair and its roaring in your ears. All summer you can ride. But it's this fall I want to talk to you about."

Cal looked at his father but said nothing.

"You know how Bellerophon was carried over hills and across the sea by his steed? Well, you can come to know just such wonders as Bellerophon, and I suspect even greater with a horse more powerful than Pegasus."

"How do you mean?"

"Education, something beyond just reading and writing here in the stone schoolhouse. You know I spoke some time back of your going to the Liberal Institute at the Union come fall?"

"Some folks think the Institute won't open again."

"Well, if it does, I want it to have Calvin Coolidge aboard."

"Why, Papa?"

"Have you and Abbie enjoyed hearing about Bellerophon, and Europa and all the Greek gods and goddesses?"

Cal nodded.

"Well, education will open up to you the whole shining world of the Greeks of 2200 years ago, then the Roman culture, from which our law takes so much. The Renaissance, Mother England, the Colonies, the great figures of our own past. You'll get an understanding of science with the great changes it's making in our lives. The great literature of our heritage, other literatures, other languages: Latin, French and Italian, perhaps. There's no end to the wonders you and Abbie will know. After the Institute I hope you'll both go to the big academy in Ludlow, Black River Academy, then perhaps on to college. It's a magnificent vista you can know — much more than the world of your father and your grandfather.

"Grandpa wanted me to be a farmer."

"I know. That's why he gave you the Lime Kiln Lot, fixed so you couldn't sell it but would have to work it yourself. Having a good education is no reason not to be a farmer. A farmer's life can be just that much broader and more wonderful with the understanding an education can give."

"You want me to be a farmer?"

"Calvin, I want you to be what *you* want to be, to follow your own God-given talents wherever they take you. Who knows . . .?"

The two sat in silence for a few moments. Then Cal said, "Here comes Abbie. I promised her I'd hunt for the peahens' nests with her."

V.

MUSIC IN THE MOUNTAINS

Life could be dull in a little town like Plymouth, with only 1400 inhabitants, if it didn't have a "Singing Class." This group interested in music, or in seeing each other, met weekly through the winter. Anybody was welcome, though the Singing Master was sometimes hard put to find things for somebody to do who couldn't even carry a tune. It was a true democracy: if the hired man had a good voice he was likely to be assigned an important solo part.

Sugaring had begun about the time Calvin's and Abbie's mother died. It provided a merciful round of activity to keep one from brooding too much. But the evenings were still a problem.

"Captain cut his fetlock on the icy crust this afternoon," Calvin volunteered as his father sat down at the supper table and asked the blessing.

"I guess it's not a good plan to take Captain out to the sugar house till this crust melts. Did you get Merrill to put some salve on it?"

Cal nodded. "He said it would be all right."

"Calvin didn't even look where Captain was going," his nine-year-old sister Abbie contributed. "Calvin's just day-dreaming all the time. Half the time he don't know when Mr. Carpenter calls on him to recite."

" 'Doesn't know,' " their father corrected his small daughter. "Calvin," he continued, turning to his son, "I know it's hard for us to get started again, but we've *got* to. Mother would want it. How about you and Abbie, and Martha if she'd like, coming with me to Singing Class tonight. You'll probably see Stella there," his father added, noting Calvin's reluctance.

"But I can't sing," Cal protested.

"That don't matter," Cousin Martha spoke up from the end of the table where she was ladling out hot stew. "You'll see lots of folks there that you like."

The vestibule of the Notch Church was already alive with people. John Coolidge was right: Stella *was* there. After all, her father, Harmon McWain, was the Singing Master. Stella could hardly miss, though it was a longish trip by pung through Frog City and the Union up to the hall at the Notch.

A preliminary chord on the organ brought an end to the buzz of conversation. Several rounds, involving everybody in one of the parts, came first. Then a couple of songs that all knew and loved to sing. Finally the group got down to business. There was a new round to learn, then the repertoire of the double quartet to support. This was followed by a romantic favorite,

> Last night the nightingale awoke me,
> Last night when all was still.

The song went on to a climax in which the soprano voices soared in "But, oh-oh, the bird was singing, my love, of you."

This was a favorite also of Mr. Carpenter's classes in the little stone school house. Recently Ernest Carpenter, the popular young teacher in the District Nine ungraded school at the Notch, had noted that Calvin would put his head down on his desk when this song came to its climax. His shoulders shook with silent sobs. Not understanding the cause for Calvin's emotion, the teacher had decided to by-pass this particular song.

Harmon McWain had no such background. The girls of the Singing Class, some of them just a couple of years older than Calvin, recognized this as the song of a love-sick swain to his lady love. They rose to full crescendo at the climax — "the bird was singing, my love, of you." Cal had identified the "you" with his mother. It was too much for him: unnoted except by his father, the boy slipped out of

the group and retreated to the relative privacy of the curtained area across from the choir.

He had hardly found a place to sit down when he became aware of another figure beyond the circle of lamplight in the front of the room. It was Stella McWain. She was crying. A hesitant voice beside her spoke softly. "Whatchuh cryin' about, Stella?"

The girl looked up into the sad eyes of her cousin, Calvin. "Oh, it's you, Calvin. My brand new hat," she sobbed. "It's Lettie's. She just bought it in Woodstock. But she couldn't wear it tonight because she's got a bad cold and couldn't come. So I got her to let me wear it."

"Well?" Cal asked, puzzled.

"I had it pinned on real tight, but when we came to the flats just beyond Frog City Papa and I had wrapped the blankets up around our faces because of the wind, and a big gust came and carried the hat away. The wind blew it over that hard crust off into the woods some place. We couldn't see where. And I had it pinned on tight, too." The girl lapsed into sobs again.

This amount of emotion over a mere hat was beyond the boy. "Was that why you didn't want to play the organ no more — any more — this evening?" He asked, after a pause, one part of this feminine mystery becoming clearer.

"Yes. It had a bird on the side of it, a beautiful bird that looked almost real. And Lettie didn't want me to take it, but Papa persuaded her. Oh, what am I going to do. Lettie will —"

A restraining hand came down on the girl's shoulder. Her father's firm but kindly voice said, "Stella, don't be silly. I'll take care of Lettie. They want you should play now."

Calvin sat for a moment considering this strange type of sadness, then drifted off to talk with Dell and Clarence Blanchard, who would probably be hatching some sort of prank he should be in on. Cal could never resist a practical joke. He was, in fact, something of a connoisseur of practical jokes, his expertise extending to the problem of a plausible alibi establishing his non-involvement. So it had been the year before when he realized that the long stove pipe crossing the school room to the chimney on the opposite side had some intriguing possibilities. He managed to persuade Dell, that master shinny-er, to climb up before school opened and pat a snowball into place on a rafter above the stove pipe. When the fire was built and the room started to heat up, the snow melted and dropped on the pipe with a fine sizzling sound. The school commissioners, called in to find the leak in the roof, stated that they "couldn't understand" how that snow got in. The roof was "as sound as a bell"!

* * *

Sugaring was really the start of spring. It came late to the mountains. One day could be biting and cold; the next, warm and full of bird songs.

"Thank God for work," John Coolidge had remarked at the time of Vikki's death. In a culture shot through with the Puritan work ethic, this sentiment, though unvoiced, was shared by his son.

"I'm going to let you plow that rye field this spring, Calvin. Remember, I promised you? Still want to try it?"

Cal nodded eagerly. "I held the plow right in line last year when you let me take the handles. The rye field's simple. Almost no stones."

John studied his son thoughtfully. "Tomorrow's the day to do it. Going to be perfect plowing weather, and we need to get the early potatoes in before the next rain. But I can't be here. I'll have Merrill help you get started. Think you can handle it all morning by yourself? Merrill's got to fix that buggy for the Franklins. He's been waiting for his new bellows for the forge. Now it's here."

The boy squared his shoulders and threw back his head. "I could have plowed that rye field last year."

The next day was as beautiful as the evening sun had predicted. The combination hired man and blacksmith — and friend of Cal and all children — was on hand to make sure that the slender youngster could manage the heavy harness. "'Twas your grandfather's love for animals that made that team so gentle," Merrill remarked. "But it ain't a real good idea to reach under Captain's belly. He might have a fly to take care of just that moment."

Calvin gave his mentor an appreciative glance. "I know it. Just didn't think you'd notice I fastened the tugs first. I won't again."

"Now remember them reins around your neck. When you want 'em to slow down, you lean back on the reins. And speak up real sharp when you want 'em to gee or haw. That's good. You won't have no trouble."

Though the handles of the plow were sometimes almost too much for the twelve-year old's slender strength, the intoxicating feeling that he was doing a man's work — and all by himself — buoyed him up. The clean brown earth as he followed in the new furrow felt pleasantly cool to his feet. The earth worms wriggled out behind him. Attracted by this free lunch, blackbirds followed at a safe distance. The plowman smelled an intoxicating fragrance compounded of springing herbage, newly-turned earth, and maple blossoms in the distance.

He was surprised that the sun stood right over his head when he finished. Unhooking the check reins, he let the team browse a moment while he surveyed his work. The dead furrow was 'most as straight as Grandpa Coolidge would have made it — well, most of its length. The successive furrows turned over as even as waves on the Reservoir — well, nearly as even anyway. He'd come out with the harrow in the afternoon. Too bad his father couldn't see how even the plowing was before the harrow smoothed it. He'd be tickled. Cal reached over and patted the sleek necks of the team, scratched them behind the ears as he'd seen Grandpa Coolidge do. Grandpa loved his horses.

As he trudged back behind the team drawing the plow on its side, a new idea came to him. Could he, after he was through with the disk harrow, get out the potato marker and run the furrows for the potatoes? He glanced at his dead furrow. No, that would be tempting fate too much. And any wobbling in the rows would show all season.

* * *

Nevertheless, this triumph of his early manhood came in handy at the Fourth of July picnic. At first he hadn't even wanted to go. But the picnic was going to be held in a beautiful stretch of woods down at the Union. Traditionally they began with a "sing," for which a wheezy portable organ was brought in. The boys took turns pumping it. After the sing and much laughter over simple jokes, there were games for the younger set down in the meadow by a smooth-flowing brook. Then mountains of food.

There was also Midge Gilson. She was the youngest of three

daughters of a well-to-do New Yorker who had built himself a remarkable house on Black Pond, up the road a piece and before you came to the Reservoir. Cal had never paid much attention to these girls, not being interested in girls and particularly not in summer people.

Midge Gilson changed all that. She was a slender, lithe girl with big brown eyes and blond hair done in a pony tail. She came over when she spotted Calvin, standing by himself as was so often the case. "Say, aren't you one of the Coolidges up at the Notch?"

Calvin nodded.

"You're Calvin Coolidge, aren't you?"

This time she got a "Yup" for answer.

"Say, you're getting good looking," she burbled on. "I never noticed it before. You must be 'bout fourteen or so, aren't you?"

"I'm thirteen today. This is my birthday."

The girl's lips parted in an appreciative smile, and her eyes sparkled. "Then this celebration is for you, your birthday party."

No response. Cal had heard this one before.

"But boys up here grow up sooner than city boys — not so?"

"Well, I dunno about that," Cal said slowly. "But I mistrust if any of those city slickers could do what I did the other day."

"I bet they couldn't. What was it you did?" The girl listened with bated breath while Calvin described his triumph with the plow, which had greatly pleased his father who had gone right out to see it. Nothing less than a feat like this could have inspired such eloquence in the boy.

"What are the names of the team, Captain and Dolly? Nice names. And you say you like to ride Captain? Say," she went on, "I'd love to see Captain. Why don't you ride him down to our place? You know where it is — on Black Pond. If you come down through the Crandall Place it's just a step, for a horse like Captain. Bet you've done it lots of times."

Cal allowed that perhaps he had.

"Then come down and show me Captain. I love horses."

* * *

John Coolidge could not have known how apt his words were when he stepped out of the blacksmith shop just in time to see Calvin riding past on Captain. "What was the name of that winged horse I used to read you and Abbie about — Pegasus?"

Calvin nodded.

"And the young man who rode him — what was his name?"

"Bellerophon."

"Yes, I couldn't think of it. Well, Pegasus took Bellerophon over land and sea, through enchanted forests and into new wonders. That's what an education does for you — opens up new wonders, worlds you'd never dreamt of. I want you to think about that as you ride along. Now that you're thirteen we ought to finish that talk about your education. I think it's Black River Academy next fall. Would you like that? Well, think about it."

But Captain-Pegasus was taking his young rider into new and enchanted lands that very day. Down through the Crandall place Pegasus flew and on past the fantastic yellow house overlooking the magic waters of Black Pond. Pegasus would have turned in at the gateway, but Bellerophon's hand on the rein failed to guide the steed to make the turn. Bellerophon had lost his nerve. So Pegasus carried Bellerophon down through the Union and back home by the Notch road.

VI

LOST IN THE WILDERNESS

John Coolidge worried about his son's depression that summer after his mother had died. Interludes like the Independence Day picnic were some help; but trips after evening chores were done, trips to his mother's grave in the little Notch cemetery, were almost constant. John Coolidge could recognize and handle his own grief, although this wasn't easy. His concern for the two children helped. But Calvin was in need of help, more than he could give, and of a different sort.

"Calvin," he began when he found the boy alone, "Calvin, I've been thinking that you need a change. You've been faithful to your mother and she loved your company. But you need a few days away from home. New scenes, new people, new things to think about. . ."

The pair lapsed into silence, each struggling with his own adjustment to what had happened. Finally his father spoke again. "You remember Moses Colburn from up Shrewsbury way? You saw him at Grandpa's funeral, but you were too young to pay much heed. How about a little trip up there, you and Dell, if he can get away? Like that idea?"

Cal looked into his father's eyes, which reflected the pain in his own. "Not 'specially," he said.

"Well, Calvin, sometimes we have to make ourselves do what's good for us. Now, as I think of it, I need a message taken up to a young man up by Patch Pond, Moses Townsend. Some papers he should sign. They're legal papers and valuable. Could you and Dell find him and then go on to the Colburns? I'll write the Colburns a note asking could you and Dell stay overnight. I don't have time to drive way up there, but I do have to go to Ludlow tomorrow for grain. I'd like you to do that legal errand for me. I'll take you as far as Tyson."

Cal nodded his head.

"The Furnace" — Tyson Furnace — was still a busy place a hundred years ago. The iron mine Cyrus Tyson had opened was at this time less productive, but there was still enough iron to make the famous Tyson stove tops. Where other iron tops on a kitchen stove would sag if the metal was allowed to get red hot, these tops stayed firm. They were therefore much in demand.

"You two boys will see lots of interesting things besides the Furnace," John Coolidge said to Calvin and Dell as they reached Tyson. "And young Moses Townsend himself is somebody to know. He's determined, that young man. He's buying the Isaac Pollard place, and perhaps some other land down by Patch Pond. You better get him to show you where Patch Pond is, too. Might like to go fishing there some time. Before you come to the place I think Townsend is buying, if you turn where I said to turn, you'll pass an old mill. Grinds most of the flour for Nineveh Village — whoa, Dolly — I want to know is it still going. After you pass the Furnace, be sure you take the left fork along Patch Brook. Then your first left when you strike open land up top of the hill. It's a whole new country for both of you. A nice big pond just beyond the Townsends'. Didn't you say you've never been beyond Patch Brook, Dell?"

"Once, with Pa, but I don't remember it too good."

"Well, Calvin's been up there, too, but he doesn't remember it either. You'll find the Colburns' place all right, Calvin, and don't forget to give them the maple sugar. Tell 'em it's Plymouth *Notch* sugar, and real special. And get them to tell you just how to find the road that comes out where I showed you at Frog City. You can't miss it. Here, don't forget your pack, Dell. And careful of those legal papers, Calvin. They're valuable."

The blast furnace was in full operation. Dark forms silhouetted against the red throat of the smelting furnace seemed to the boys like figures they'd heard about at church.

"Think that's the kind of place Reverend Meeker was talking about last Sunday, only that was bigger, of course?" Dell asked. "That big fellow over there could be the devil. His face is black enough. Look at him." The boys crowded closer, till the big man, who seemed to be in charge, shouted something at the young visitors and made a motion with his arm. The boys got the message and left.

Each pool on Patch Brook seemed better for trout than the one before. "Wish we'd brought some fishline," Dell remarked.

"Ehyuh. But I guess Papa thought we might have trouble finding Mr. Townsend." With this thought in mind, the boys quickened their pace up the old wagon road which paralleled the brook.

"This must be the left turn Papa told us about," Cal pointed ahead to a well-traveled road branching off to the left. "It's on cleared land and it's level."

As they made the left turn, they came on Patch Brook again. But here instead of the tumbling mountain torrent, flashing down over boulders into rock-girt pools, this was a wide, placid stream, held back by a dam.

"Your pa spoke of a grist mill. Remember? There it is." Dell pointed to an ancient moss-grown gray building on the far side of the dam. Between the building and the dam there was a spill-way, and just beyond a sluice full of rushing water. Then a large paddle wheel, attached to the building.

"Aw, it ain't running," Dell said. "Water's going through the sluiceway instead of over the wheel. Bet they's some good horn-pout in that there little pond," he concluded.

"Yuh. P'raps we can come back. But we've got to find this Mr. Townsend. Papa said we'd find him most likely at the Pollard farm down the road a piece."

"Somebody's hammering," Dell remarked. "Hear it?"

"It's over there, upper side of the road. There's a house."

An old man in faded gray overalls was repairing a carriage shed attached to the house. He paused as the boys came up to him. "Be you lookin' for anyone in perticerler or jist out takin' the air?"

"We're lookin' for a Moses Townsend," Cal replied.

"Mose? Well he aint here. Mebbee he otter be, 'cause this here shed is his'n, and I got a couple questions t'ask him."

"Where's he at?" Cal asked, slipping easily into the vernacular.

"Mose? Most likely over to his wife's place, the old Hays place up the rud a piece. Know the place?"

"No, we've never been up here before," Cal answered.

"You come up from the Furnace, did you?"

Calvin nodded.

"All right. Go back to where you turned off the Patch Brook road and keep on along of the road till you come to the Four Corners. Straight through the Corners would take you to Hortonville. But you turn right, and foller the road matter of a mile or so further to where the old Crown Point Road crosses. Jist down that road, oh, a stone's throw, you'll see the Hays place. Most likely you'll find him there. When you see him, you'll be a-lookin' at the eighth wonder of the world."

"What's that — 'eighth wonder of the world'?" Cal asked.

"Well, m'boy, when you see a man as bought more'n a thousand acres stretchin' from the Crown Point Road clear down to Patch Pond and clear around it to the Frank Hastings place, you're looking at somebody as has big idees." The old man spat a line of tobacco juice into a pile of shavings and sat down on a saw horse.

"Thousand acres?" Dell asked in amazement. "Can he farm all that?"

"Nope," the old man said in a tone of finality. "And a lot of it can't be farmed. Just along the shore of the pond. I sez to Mose, I sez, 'Mose, what you want all that land fer? What you got along the shore o' Patch Pond ain't no good for nothin'. Can't plant pertaters in it; can't do nothin' with it.' "

" 'Well, that's all right,' he sez. 'Some day land along a lake shore's goin' to be valuable.' " The old man threw back his head and gave a cackling laugh. "I tell you, the man's tetched in the haid."

Calvin had listened thoughtfully. "Maybe the pond's special. My father said it wasn't far from here. Is it on our way to the Hays?"

"Nope: t'other direction, jist down this rud a spell. But you kin see it, then cut over through them woods, across Farmer Brook and that medder to the Patch Brook rud again. You'll be pretty nigh the Corners I tole you about."

When they found the Pond, the two boys stood for a while looking out over its wooded shores, an expanse bigger, it seemed, than the familiar Woodward Pond. Dell spoke first: "Bet they's some good bull-head in them little coves."

Calvin seemed to come out of a trance. "Beautiful. Mama would have loved it," he said quietly. "She loved sunsets, and water, and spruce trees like those over yonder. I sure want to see this Moses Townsend."

The old man's directions were good. The boys found the old Hays place with no trouble, a big unpainted frame house with a wilderness of hollyhocks up against the front, reminding Cal of his grandparents' place. Beyond the house were the barns, and a wide sweep of meadow running across to a fringe of woods. But in the meadow, fairly near the house, a hay wagon was being loaded. An elderly man was pitching forks full of hay up to a tall, lanky young man with a mustache and a sandy beard. Beside the growing hayload, a young girl with a bull rake was cleaning up the wisps of hay left when a haycock was pitched onto the load. She it was who first noticed the two boys striding toward them. "Hello, boys," she called out. "Looking for someone? You're John Coolidge's boy, ain't you?" she asked, as the boys came up to her. "You've growed a lot since I seen you, but I reco'nized you right off."

"Yes, me and Dell here, Dell Ward, my father sent us up with some papers. We're looking for Moses Townsend."

The tall, lanky young man sprang down from the wagon. "I'm Moses Townsend. You say your father sent something up for me?"

"Yes, legal papers. But before I give them to you I was to ask, Are you still figgering to buy the Isaac Pollard place?"

The young man chuckled. "I wouldn't be picking up this here hay to put into a Pollard barn if I wasn't buying it. We're planning to live

there come winter."

While the young man studied the papers, the older man came over to where his daughter stood chatting with the boys. "Can't keep up with Mose; glad to have some excuse to rest." He wiped his brow with the back of his arm. "So you're John Coolidge's son," he said, extending his hand. "Glad to know you. I met you 'bout five or maybe six years ago, but you was a little shaver, 'bout so high. And what's your friend's name? He a neighbor? You're a long way from the Notch."

"Yes, you must be tired," the girl remarked, as if she'd just thought of the matter of distance. "We'll be having lunch right soon now. Come and set with us."

This was the formula for inviting one to a meal, and Calvin recognized it as such, but he said promptly, "We got our own provender, put up for two days."

Just then a farm bell on the end of the house clanged, and a moment later a stout woman with glasses, her bare arms wrapped in a large apron, called out to the group, "Didn't know you was right here by the door, like. Everything's ready. These some visitors? Bring them in."

It was a good hearty farm dinner, the big meal of the day.

"Look, you boys, save your provender for later on," Mrs. Hays said. "We got a plenty."

Mr. Hays spoke up. "One thing a farmer has is plenty to eat. May not have much money, and what with prices the way they be, and that bunch in Washington, it's gettin' worse. But we got lots to eat — and plenty of wood for heat. What more does a man want?"

"Well, a woman wants new clothes," his daughter suggested timidly.

"You mean she can't make 'em?" Mr. Hays asked, looking up from his big mug of quite mature cider. "What's the sheep for, and the spinnin' wheel?" he asked, winking at the boys.

* * *

"Nice people, the Hayses," the two boys agreed as they set out at last for the Colburns, to which place they had just been given ample directions.

"I don't think Moses Townsend is 'tetched in the haid' the way that old coot said," Dell observed.

"Course he's not. Pa would say that old feller just don't understand Mr. Townsend. The way I figger it, Mr. Townsend worked hard for twenty years, as he said, to get the money to start buying land. Now he's got enough money to start, and doesn't have to live with Mrs. Townsend's folks any longer. I don't blame Mr. Townsend. Did you notice the way Mr. Hays threw out that same thing about buying land on a pond?"

* * *

The Colburns welcomed the two dusty travelers as the cherished guest-friends they were. "You boys are all sweat," Mrs. Colburn said. "Calvin, your shirt's just dripping. Come out here to the pump and get washed up." Mrs. Colburn bustled around finding towels. "I never see such heat," she remarked. "The boys are out git'n' in wood. They'll be along by the time you've freshened up."

The boys, Jim somebody and his brother Jack, were working through the summer for the Colburns. They were glad to see the travelers from the Notch. New friends to talk to, new companions to help with chores — these were rarities. "Come help us feed out," the two boys suggested. "We got some good young stock coming up," Jim said. The four trooped out to the barnyard, and into the largest barn Cal had ever seen.

During the evening meal Mrs. Colburn plied the guests with questions. "Your grandmother still keep up the Galusha Coolidge place?" she asked. "I heard she keeps it just like it was when Galusha was there. A good hired man, I guess."

"What's your father's name, Dell? — Adelbert, that your real name?" Mr. Colburn asked.

"Nope. Just Dell," the boy answered. "My brother's Oric Ward. We're working up the road a piece from the Coolidges, Hall place, living with the Ayres."

"Your father still running the store, Calvin?" Mr. Colburn asked.

"Dell," Mrs. Colburn said, "This blueberry pie I made just this afternoon. Pail of blueberries from blueberry hill."

"You and Calvin'll have to get up here next summer come blueberry time," Jim said, "and we'll go berrying. Bring along cupla big pails and we'll fill 'em up."

"They's other folks like them blueberries," young Jack added, grinning. "Some big furry folks with claws."

"Bears?" Calvin asked, raising his head.

"Yuh, black bears."

The boys slept in one end of the attic. They were up at day-break to help Jim and Jack with chores. The Colburns' cattle were all Jerseys. "Your grandpa Coolidge liked pure-bred stock," Mr. Colburn remarked. "We got some good Jerseys from Pomfret. Grades, but real good. Figgering to raise us some mighty fine heifers along of the Hays bull.."

"You didn't see Old Stormer, did you? They keep him tied in most of the while," Jack remarked.

* * *

Jim and Jack had come out some distance with their new friends. "Look," Jim said, before they parted. "The road Mr. Colburn gave you, down through Frog City, that's as crooked as a dog's hind leg. Why not see some good wild country and go on to the North Shrewsbury Road, then follow that down to the Union?"

"Yuh," Jack broke in. "That trail we took when we was coon huntin'. You can't miss it."

"All right, Jack, let me tell them," Jim said sharply, asserting his rights as the elder brother. "You go back to the Four Corners, then turn left. You follow this road past the Crown Point road. Then when it takes a sharp bend to the right, like so," he drew the road in the dust with a stick, "where it turns sharp right, you keep straight ahead. It's an old logging road for a piece. You cross a brook, see, then the old road gives out. That's where you catch the trail. It goes right along the top of the ridge and clear over to the Northam road.

We bin over there not long ago — well, last year, and it was plain. You can't miss it."

Feeling that they'd made a couple of new friends, Calvin and Dell trudged along eager to see this new and dramatic country Jim and Jack had told about. "You can get a couple real good views out from up there," Jack had added.

The logging road was no problem. When it ended they picked up the trail Jim and Jack had described. But it got fainter as they hurried along. Finally it gave out altogether.

"I think it's this way," Cal said. "Come on."

After a while Dell asked, "Are you sure we're on the trail?"

"I guess so. Look, some of these yellow birch leaves that have fallen; they make the path show up better. See it ahead there?"

"Let me look." Dell parted the bushes up ahead, studied the ground a little while, then said in a dull voice, "that's a deer track. See up there? It turns sharp down, and the trail Jim told about they said ran right along the ridge."

"Well, why don't we just go on straight when that deer trail turns down? We'll pick up the trail again. Must run right along here."

But it didn't. And the "ridge" wasn't just a simple spine that one could follow and be sure he was right. It was interrupted by a couple of high hills. Then a deep ravine would cut through beside a hill, and they had to get across that. It was unnerving.

Dell finally put his fears into words. "We're lost," he said. "This ain't no little ridge, like them boys said. And this woods goes on for miles and miles. And the bears — there must be lots of them up here. I've seen bear turds cupla times. Why did we —"

For a moment panic seized Calvin, too. Fear, stark fear of something he had not let himself consider before overwhelmed him. What should they do? They could wander in these trackless wilds and not be found for days. They could die here.

"Steady, now, steady. Easy does it." It was his grandfather's voice. Calvin had not been sure at the time whether Grandpa was speaking to him, the little six-year-old, as the small grandson tried to clamber up to stand behind his grandfather on the horse's broad back, or whether Grandpa was "gentling" the Morgan on which he was sitting. But no matter: "Easy does it." It was good advice and he was thankful for Grandpa.

"Listen, Dell, let's not get excited. Let's sit down right here and eat lunch. Then we'll decide what to do."

Dell had no appetite for lunch, nor had Calvin.

"I don't know about you," Dell said after a while, "But I'm scairt. I bin lost before, but not in country we never bin in a tall. Nobody'd even know where to look for us."

"If we both git scairt," Cal said, "We'll sure be in trouble."

"Can we find our way back, the way we came?"

"P'raps. But if we did, it would be too late to take the Frog City road and get home before dark. Look, Dell, it's reasonable: if we stay on the high land and keep going, cutting around the ravines but still heading north, we've *got* to come out on the Northam road that runs down to the Union. We're probly just an hour or two from it now."

"Maybe, but I'm scairt. I never slept out in my life. Is there wolves here, d'yuh think?"

"We're not going to sleep out. Wanna finish this piece of cheese? I can't eat any more."

"I don't want it. I jest wanna get home."

"Well, once we are over this next ravine and head up that hill, we'll be gettin' along."

"That hill's probly bigger'n the one we just climbed, and more boulders."

"Then save your breath for climbing."

The next few hours were grim. Calvin watched the shadows grow longer. The woods were still thick and the land had leveled off so there was no ridge to follow. Did Papa say the moss grows on the north side of trees, or was it the south side? he asked himself. Dell had fallen behind. Calvin began to feel some of the deep discouragement that made Dell's footsteps lag. Oh, if he'd only listened to his father and kept to the safe way, down the Frog City road and along the route from Ludlow. Would they have to spend the night out in the woods, a cold night, and with no blankets? What would they do? His own pace began to slacken. "Hey, Dell. Where are you? Let's not lose each other."

"I'm here," a faint voice called.

Calvin waited for his chum to catch up, trying to suppress his own mounting fears.

"Look, Dell, there's nothing to do but go ahead, trying to keep due north. We have to find that road before dark. We —"

Suddenly Dell held up his hand. "Did you hear it?" he asked, his eyes opening wide.

"What was it?" Cal asked. "A bear?"

"No, a horse whinnied. There it is again. Come on." Dell started to run.

"Wait up, Dell, I — can't — go so fast. Maybe I should have eaten more."

"Here it is," Dell shouted back. "Here's a road. And a cupla horses just been by. That's what we heard. They's some fresh horse buns."

Both boys stood in the road, looking at each other. Never had they realized how wonderful it could be just to stand in a road, just to look each way on a road, each way, but particularly down toward Plymouth Union.

"I'm hungry," Dell announced as they started down the road.

"So'm I. Let's walk on till we find a brook or a spring or something. I'm thirsty too."

"So'm I. Never knew I could be so thirsty. It was that dry bread, and the cheese and the apple butter Martha put in. Let's eat now."

"Yuh, let's. We can find a brook later."

As dusk came on, two tired boys, tired but happy, and no longer either hungry or thirsty, came down a winding road into Plymouth Union. They passed the Liberal Institute; they went by the Browns, then the Moores on their left, and headed up the steep hill to the Notch.

About half way up the hill, they sighted a buggy coming toward them. It was Calvin's father. "We got kind of uneasy about you two when you didn't show up for supper. So I thought I'd come down to meet you. Tired, boys?"

"No," Cal said. "Not now. And we found Moses Townsend. He's

buying the Pollard place. I gave him the papers you had for him, and he signed that thing you wanted him to sign if he was buying. It's all here in the pack."

"Well, we're mighty glad you're back. What took you so long, Dell?"

"We came a new way", Dell said, and lapsed into silence.

VII

"GO UP HIGHER" —

The County Court at Woodstock was stuffy on this hot September day. The subject under discussion, something about land rights and rights of way, this was stuffy, too. Calvin loved these trips to the county seat with his father, but parts of the trip could be boring. John Coolidge noticed his son's restlessness. "You don't have to stay here in Court and listen if you don't want to." His father leaned over the bench where Calvin was sitting. "Go on downstairs if you wish. Get outside. Only don't go beyond ear-shot. I don't know when this will end, but I don't want to have to hunt you up when I'm ready to go."

The big downstairs hall was cool, and there were people passing by, something to watch. Calvin found a seat on a big box of books which was waiting to be unpacked for the Court library. His unaccustomed shoes hurt his feet.

"You John Coolidge's boy, be yuh?"

Calvin looked up at a large man in tattered overalls. His blue denim shirt was open at the neck. The boy nodded.

"Well, boy — Calvin, ain't it? — we think a lot of your father 'round here. He ain't all fuss an' feathers like most of them fellers you see givin' speeches. Fact, he ain't much on speeches, but when there's somethin' needs figurin' out, he thinks it through and says it right out like it is. Honest as the day is long. And he's got courage, too. Come hell or high water, if'n the thing is right, he'll stick up for it no matter what. Kind of like a bantie rooster, he is: no matter what the big politicians say, he'll stick to the facts and do what's right. Not to say your pa, a big tall man like him, is a bantie rooster, 'ceptin' he's got guts like a bantie."

A couple of loiterers had stopped to listen. "John Coolidge, Chet?" one of them asked. "Yuh, he's got what it takes, but mostly he doesn't have to get tough. Folks respect him. He's quiet and friendly."

The other man spoke up. "Yuh, he's friendly. They's lots o' folks all over this county he's done things for and never charged 'em a cent. Ezry, 'member the time at Plymouth Town Meet'n' when we was afraid the voters was goin' to load us with a big debt to fix the Pinney Holler road? I knew John wanted it done; he saw it was needed; but when it come to vot'n, he didn't stand up. If'n he had, it would prob'ly a brot enuf others in to swing the vote. He knew they was folks there as couldn't stand the extry tax. And so the motion didn't pass."

"Young man," the first loiterer spoke up. "You gonna be a real leader like your pa — and like your Grampa Galusha Coolidge? You couldn't do no better. We need more men like them. Come on, Chet. We'll treat you to something to wet your whistle."

The threesome strolled out. Lost in thought, Calvin sat where he was till the court was over and his father separated himself from the stream of people coming down the broad staircase. He came over to his son. "Too long a session. You hungry? We can sample Martha's lunch on the way home."

As the boy unsnapped the mare from the hitching post in front of the Court House, and climbed in beside his father, John Coolidge turned to look at his son. "Glad we laid in those groceries before Court took up. I didn't know it would last so long. Did you follow it at all?"

"What was it about?" Cal asked. "I couldn't make much of it."

"Well, it was a hard case to settle. What we call a 'rolling corner.' Man who accused his neighbor of moving the corner. Hard to prove he hadn't, for there were no witnesses."

"Witnesses? Wouldn't he do it at night and by himself?"

His father chuckled. "Often at an important corner they set in a couple of posts near the main one to serve as 'witnesses' that the main post is right. But I convinced the Court — the judge — that with the post there, where it is, the piece is a good squared-off rectangle. To move it out of line destroys the proper balance in both parcels. That's what I had that big drawing for, showing the two pieces. They took my word for it. See anybody downstairs you liked better than yourself?"

Calvin smiled faintly. "There was a man down there, big fat man with a red face. He thinks a lot of you."

"Big? Ruddy complexion?"

"Yes. Couple of other fellows came along. They called him Chet."

"Oh, must be Chester Parsons. I helped him once. Right of adverse possession."

"What's that?"

"Well, there isn't any such law in Vermont, but in Massachusetts, where the Coolidges came from back in the 1700's, if a man builds a shelter of any sort, a permanent dwelling, no matter how simple, on a piece of land he doesn't own, he can establish 'squatters' rights' if he stays a number of years and if the owner never challenges him or chases him off."

"What did this have to do with Mr. Parsons?"

"Oh, yes. He built himself a log cabin, messy, but it served his needs. Edge of the far pasture of another man's land. The owner found out about it and warned him off. Chester didn't move, so the owner sued him. Poor fellow, he couldn't understand that he was doing any damage, excepting it was messy all around the cabin. I was able to convince the Court that Chet didn't mean to do anything wrong. He just didn't understand the law."

"Didn't Mr. Parsons want to get married and live in a house in the Village?"

"Chet's not the marrying kind. And he doesn't much like people. I knew an old couple who needed a good strong man around now and then and I persuaded them to let Chet have an old milk house that wasn't being used. But he left so much litter around that they couldn't stand it. I got them to help him build another cabin, off in the woods at the upper end of their property. He stops in on the couple two or three times a week, and everybody's happy."

"How did you learn all this about the right of— what was it? Did you study law?"

"Right of adverse possession? Well, no, I didn't ever study *law*, but I studied history and literature and math and logic — and these taught me how to dig out from law books any points I needed as a sheriff."

"These things you studied at Black River Academy did that for you?"

"That's right. It's a good school. Remember Pegasus and Bellerophon? That's what an education can do. Opens up new paths, roads you didn't know existed, and shows you how to discover still other roads. I think you should go there, come fall. But like Dolly, here, you can lead her to water but you can't make her drink."

They drove along a while in silence. "Getting hungry?" John Coolidge asked finally. "Where did you put that lunch Martha made for us?"

Calvin leaned over and brought out from under the seat a parcel done up in dark brown wrapping paper. "I'm glad she put in plenty of cheese," the boy remarked.

"Real Plymouth cheese," his father said with a note of pride. "That cheese factory I want to buy may pay better than the store, if I can get a couple of neighbors convinced."

"If I go to Black River Academy this fall, can I come home weekends?"

"Well, probably. If I'm free I can come down and get you, and take you back Sunday afternoon. If it should happen I can't be free, there's always Shank's mare. You can do it on foot in three hours. Twelve miles, or thereabouts. But mostly I can come down for you. I'd like to do that."

The pair fell silent again, stuffed with Martha McWain's ample lunch.

Finally Cal broke the silence. "Do you think Moses Townsend went to the Academy?"

"Well, could be. He came from Pittsfield, if I remember right. The questions he asked — on that sheet of paper he sent along with the signed documents — they showed both a good mind and a mind that had had some training. You admired him, didn't you. What impressed you so about him?"

Cal thought a moment. "Well, he can see ahead. He knows what he wants and he goes after it. All those people laughing at him for buying so much land — and around a big pond at that — they didn't bother him one bit. And he's not afraid of hard work — likes it, I'd say."

"He must, to take on a thousand acres. How much would you say was forest, and how much pasture?"

Calvin thought a while. "There's a big lot of pasture across the road from the Pollard house where we found the old carpenter. Might be a hundred acres or more. I didn't take much notice till I met Moses himself; then I tried to remember. Then there was woods, a thick stand of spruce and pine along that pond. And where we crossed from the pond back to the Hortonville road, that was all meadow, thirty acres or more, higher part of it in potatoes. He'll have to keep after that brook so it don't — doesn't — overflow. But it's good land, 'most as good as the Lime Kiln Lot, 'cept it's up higher and may not have as long a growing season."

John Coolidge chuckled. "You'd make a good farmer, I can see that. But it's not just that you like the way Moses Townsend has picked good land, and a lot of it. I reckon you like a man that thinks big, and Moses certainly does."

"And if he's had the Academy," Calvin observed, "then if he wants, he can do other things too. He'll have some other — what was the word you used?"

"Options? Yes, you're right. But looks to me, the way that young man's starting out, he plans to be a farmer, and a real good one. And since he's picked one of the Hays girls — or she's picked him — I'd say there was good stock there to start with. And that's important. Nothing more important than having a good wife."

There was silence again. Finally, as if summarizing the conversation, Cal remarked: "That pond he got with his land — it's so beautiful. Could we go up and see it again? Take along a picnic maybe, on the way down to Ludlow for grain?"

"Sometime we'll have to make a day of it, p'raps see Mr. Townsend, too."

As they crossed the first bridge up from Bridgewater Corners, John Coolidge spoke again. "Remember last year about this time, when we stopped in on the Hemenways in Ludlow? Rufus is a little older than you, but you two hit it off all right. Why don't we invite him up here for Battle of Bennington Day. He goes to the Academy and can tell you all about it. If he stayed on the rest of the week, he could help you and Merrill finish up that corn. It's getting bad."

"I shouldn't of went with you this morning. Merrill's working all alone."

"'Shouldn't have gone' — but Merrill doesn't mind. He works alone in the blacksmith shop."

"And Rufus could help me with my swimming."

"Every afternoon, after you've done your stint in the corn."

* * * *

It was the first time Dell Ward had met Rufus Hemenway. Besides being a little older than Dell, the boy was so far ahead of both Dell and Calvin that Calvin was painfully aware of it. On the way down to Mr. Woodward's pond Rufus spoke lovingly of wanting to go to see the parade in Bennington, part of the celebration of the Battle of Bennington, which, Rufus pointed out, was actually fought over the border in New York State. "But now they have a lot of fellows from the Civil War. They ride in open phaetons with red, white and blue pon-pons on the horses' heads. It's real smart."

"Why didn't you go down this year?" Cal asked. "Wait," he added. "We turn off here to Bishops'. It's the best swimmin' hole. That way goes past the Crandalls' and down to the Union."

"I didn't go to Bennington 'cause it's hard to get there," Rufus replied. "From Ludlow you have to go to Rutland. Then wait for another train to get on down to Bennington. Takes most a whole day. Coming back's worse. 'Most easier to get to Hubbardton."

"Hubbardton?" Cal asked.

"Yuh, a big battle fought there in the Revolution. Haven't you heard of it? We read about it in our history book."

"I think I've heard my father speak of it," Cal replied lamely.

"Aren't you going in, Dell?" Rufus asked, seeing the farm boy sit down to watch while Calvin and Rufus stripped off their overalls and shirts.

"Dell doesn't swim," Cal explained. "He doesn't like the water."

"Doesn't like the water?" Rufus asked in surprise. "Mostly the same water we have down in Ludlow. We all swim in the Black River, and that has a current. Come on in. What're you scairt of?"

Dell shook his head again. "Water's too cold — and they's snakes under the banks."

"Fooey," Rufus responded as his body cleft the water in a shallow dive from the shore.

Calvin waded in, but he *did* swim.

"Look, Calvin, put your head down in the water. Do the side stroke. See? One ear underwater. It's faster. Bunch of us fellows go down to the river every day after school."

The two swimmers sat on the shore and chatted while they dried off in the warm sun.

"You read about Hubbardton in your history book?" Cal asked. "What other books do you read?"

"All kinds of books. Right now I'm reading a lot of Poe, Edgar Allan Poe. 'The Purloined Letter,' 'The Pit and the Pendulum' —"

"Who's he?" Dell asked belligerently.

"Modern writer, and a great poet. You know 'The Raven', don't you Cal? We had to learn it at school."

"Probably I do," Cal said defensively. "How does it start?"

Rufus cleared his throat, then began in his best declamatory voice,

"Once upon a midnight dreary,
While I pondered weak and weary,
Over many a volume of forgotten lore,
While I nodded, nearly napping,
Suddenly there came a tapping,
As of someone gently rapping, rapping at my chamber door."

Then, warming up to his subject, Rufus went on, bringing out the refrain with exaggerated art,

"Quoth the Raven, Never more."

Calvin had meanwhile been having his own reaction to the refrain: never more would the little stone schoolhouse at the Notch satisfy him. To be a part of this magic place in Ludlow he would conquer his shyness of strangers.

"Hoh, we have lots of other subjects we study," Rufus responded to Calvin's question. "There's math, declamation, rhetoric, lots of stuff. We learn lots of poems even better than 'The Raven'."

Rufus was glad to stay the rest of the week. He hadn't been in the country, not long enough at any rate, to get the feel of it, and he didn't mind spending the mornings with Cal and Dell Ward and Merrill in the corn field. With just a little instruction from Merrill, the town boy learned what weeds to cover, what to pull out, and how to mound up the earth just enough around each hill to hold the stalks upright in a wind storm. What he lacked in skill he made up in a subtle assertion of his own superiority as a "town" boy. Merrill, who shod horses and beat out parts for broken down mowers when there was business, and doubled as Grandma Coolidge's hired man at slack times — Merrill, who lacked any book learning but was gifted with a sensitivity to the feelings of others — kept Rufus from getting too obnoxious. Merrill also slowed his own pace to stay abreast of Cal, whose small stature and slender build, inherited from his grandfather Moor, kept him at times from working with quite the speed of the others. So the week passed, Dell increasingly disgusted with the visitor, so that he found cleaning up that needed doing on his uncle's hay fields and came over less often to see Calvin, who was more and more determined to follow Rufus to Ludlow, come fall. In fact, a talk with his father elicited the possibility that Calvin might even room with the Hemenways, thus being from the start with people he knew.

When John Coolidge took their guest back down to Ludlow with Calvin, they talked it over with Mrs. Hemenway, who allowed she had an extra room Calvin could use.

Cal hurried over to tell his grandmother the exciting news, beginning with the first day of the Hemenway visit. "When we went in swimming," Calvin confided, "Dell Ward just sat like a bump on a log and watched us. Said there were snakes in the water. I was ashamed of him."

"Well, Dell isn't venturesome. But he has some very fine qualities. One is loyalty to a friend. He'd never desert you, Calvin. And he's got a way with horses — and oxen — that is something you can't learn from books. And he's generous. Remember the story we read in Sunday School a couple weeks ago, about the man invited to a wedding feast? Jesus was speaking about folks that try to put themselves higher than others. Here it is in Luke. Remember the advice our Lord gave his listeners: 'When thou art bidden, go and sit down in the lowest room; that when he that bade thee cometh, he will say, "Friend, go up higher."'"

The old lady looked into her grandson's inquiring blue eyes: "I'm only saying, Calvin, whatever happens to you, whatever you achieve through hard work, don't look down on old friends who may take another way. They're no different from you: we're all God's children."

"Then why is it you always stop me when I say 'ain't', and 'was' when it ought to be 'were'?"

"That's a different matter. When we have some schooling, we see how beautiful our language is, and how it ought to go. We become stewards of the language. If we didn't try to speak it as it ought to be, it would gradually change. It would break off into all sorts of little branches, till finally the people of Ludlow wouldn't understand the people of Plymouth, and neither could follow a man from Woodstock. But this doesn't mean we're better as *people*, does it? Some of these people here in Plymouth, including Dell, are among the finest you'll ever meet: honest, hard-working, kind. Like Merrill. He never had any education, and he isn't always a good steward of the language, but he's kind and sensitive and upright. You'll never meet a better man. Like your father. Like your grandfather. Try to be like Merrill and your father and your grandfather — all fine men."

They sat there in the waning light of the western window, silent. Calvin thought of the little trip he would make in the dusk when he left Grandma's to sit for a while by his mother's grave, and think.

"My mother was like that, too," Cal said finally. "She was loving. She loved everyone, and everybody loved her."

"Yes, Calvin," his grandmother said, getting up and patting the boy's shoulder. "You have some wonderful forebears. Remember when you go to the Academy, and I suppose Abbie will go there too in a couple of years, whatever you do and achieve, it's your forebears who are speaking through you. They were not people who were stuck up. They always used their talents and what education they had in public service, to help people who weren't so fortunate. Good bye, dear. And come over often. We'll talk some more about the Academy."

VIII

BLACK RIVER ACADEMY

It was a gray Sunday afternoon in early February of the year 1886. The temperature was well below freezing. Calvin and his father, both well tucked in with blankets in the open traverse sleigh, were on their way down the Plymouth Valley to Ludlow and Black River Academy. In the straw of the sleigh floor behind them were Calvin's two small handbags and a bull calf which John Coolidge would leave with the Ludlow stationmaster to be put aboard the midnight train to Boston.

As usual when John Coolidge and his son were going somewhere, Calvin probably driving, the father took the opportunity to break the long periods of silence with bits of sage advice and accounts of what his own boyhood had been like, or stories of Grandpa Galusha Coolidge, noted among more important achievements for his love of practical jokes.

"I can almost wish I were going back with you to the Academy, Calvin. We had some good times there. I used to listen, before I went myself, to your grandmother's stories of her life at the Academy. I guess young folks are much the same always. But with all of us, and with most of the boys and girls that go there now, the main purpose was study: to get the education which gives you freedom, that opens doors, shows you new paths, more options, as I've often said."

"Did Grampa Coolidge go to the Academy, too?" Cal asked. "He never spoke of it."

"No, he didn't, and so certain paths were not open for him. But look at what he did with his life. The Coolidge Farm is still one of the best in the whole Township of Plymouth."

"I know. And he was proud of being a good farmer."

"He always said that farming was a man's rightful occupation. I think he was disappointed when I didn't choose to be a farmer."

"He hoped that I would follow him," Cal observed. "That's why he gave me the Lime Kiln Lot in his will, with that — that — what was it you called it?"

His father chuckled. "An entailment, so you couldn't sell it, nor could creditors ever take it away from you. He figured that would give you a start in farming and keep you going till you could take over his farm too."

"Why didn't you choose to be a farmer?"

"Well, other paths were open to me, as I said, through education. Business and trade always attracted me, so I followed my own talents — as you will do."

"You don't want me to be a farmer?"

There was a pause. "Calvin, I never said that, nor do I feel that way. I expect you will follow your own bent, whatever it may be. An education opens up many possibilities, as you know. You'll be on your own now, able to choose for yourself. The courses you take will be mainly your own option."

"This first half year?"

"Not so much this term. You'll follow the prescribed course for new students. But next fall you'll have the background to make your own choices. That's what distinguishes us from the animals: freedom of will. You've always wanted to see Boston. This calf here behind us will get to Boston before you do, but he has no choice in the matter, and he won't like what he finds when he gets there. You'll get there too, but later, and as a matter of free choice, and equipped with a good education — college too, it may be — and you'll like what you find there. Remember, the calf will get there first. But through the wise choices which freedom of will can give us; through patience and determination, you will be ready to make things happen there as you'd like them to."

"Grandma's a great one on patience. She's always talking about how Grandpa would put seed in the ground, then have the patience to wait for it to come up and grow — what was it she says — from the Bible? — First the blade, then the ear — something like that."

" 'First the blade, then the ear, after that the full corn in the ear'. Was that it?"

"Yes, but it doesn't just grow. We had to do a lot to that early flint corn to get it to ripen before frost."

Cal's father chuckled. "Planted late. That was my fault. Shows I'm really not a farmer. Your grampa would have got that corn in just at the right moment. He used to say the wood we cut in the winter for next winter's fires, and for sugaring, the Lord went on seasoning and drying that wood no matter what we did. We couldn't hurry its drying; we had to have patience."

"But it cured better if it was covered from the snow and stacked so the air could get at it."

Father Coolidge chuckled again. "Guess that's freedom of choice, for us, to put it under cover where the Lord could cure it better. We don't have to go clear into Ludlow. This road down to the bridge is plowed all right. Turn here. We'll catch the Weston Road just over the bridge. Then left down to Pleasant Street. As for stacking wood, that can illustrate determination, as well as choice and patience. I remember one year when I was pretty well grown. We'd got up a lot of wood for sugaring and Grampa left it to me to draw it in. We had a good heavy snowfall before I got around to it. So the wood was pretty well covered. But I'd promised to do it, so it was my duty. If I wanted a thing, I went after it; if it was my duty, like a promise, I did it no matter what. I never ran out on an obligation or a promise, or a determination. There's Rufus and I guess the Brown boy, Henry, I think it is. See them out by the Hemenway barn?"

Two boys, stockier than Calvin, but around his age, saw the approaching sleigh and tied the horse they had brought out for water. They came bounding over the wide lawn to the Hemenway driveway just as Calvin and his father turned in at the drive. A motherly woman of ample proportions opened the door onto the porch as Calvin brought Dolly to a stop and wound his reins around the whipstock. The two boys, each with one of Calvin's handbags, led the way to a cheery upstairs room.

"I'm sure Calvin should be comfortable here," Mrs. Hemenway said as she followed the three boys and Mr. Coolidge up the stairs. "This hall is always warm from the stove in the living room and the kitchen stove, and if Calvin leaves his door open he'll be plenty warm to study there. Rufus has this room across the way. Used to be our room when my husband Rufus was alive."

"Well, son," John Coolidge said when he had inspected the room and watched the boys help his son unpack, "I guess I'll be going along down to the station so I can get home before dark. You'll be snug and warm here, and Rufus and Henry will get you started at the Academy tomorrow. Remember what I said about moving that sugarhouse wood in the snow." He extended his hand to his son, who shook it gravely. A parting pat on the back was the only show of affection allowed by New England custom. "Don't come down. You'll want to get better acquainted with the boys. And Mrs. Hemenway and I have a little business to do downstairs."

The Black River Academy building in 1886 was a big frame building on a knoll overlooking the Ludlow valley. Everything about the school was strange. It was built of wood instead of stone, like the little one-room schoolhouse at the Notch; there were about 125 students instead of the twenty to thirty Calvin was used to. And the boys and girls seemed to be all of an age, the early teens. Even the smell of the place, and the creaky wooden floors, were different. Before Calvin had a chance to sort out these impressions, Rufus and Henry took him, as had been agreed, to the office of the Principal, George Sherman. Mr. Sherman was a tall, slender man, with a sandy mustache and steel-rimmed glasses. He had a pleasant, offhand way about him that Calvin liked. They chatted a minute or two about the Hemenways, and Mrs. Hemenway, of whom Mr. Sherman evidently had a high opinion.

"Most of the 'freshman' courses, as we call them, you can easily catch up with; but French you probably will do better to start next

fall with the new class. Rufus and Henry, I think, are in that beginning class now." Mr. Sherman flicked over the pages of a notebook on his desk. "Yes, they're with this year's starting group. Hard to begin a new language after the rest have caught on." He smiled at Calvin. "You'll do better to wait on that one."

Calvin came to life. "If Rufus and Henry are taking it now, I can prob'ly get some help with the sounds. Couldn't I start now and get up before milking time to study?"

Mr. Sherman beamed through his glasses at the boy. "What time would that be?" he asked.

"Why, milking time's four o'clock; and before that would be about three."

"Wouldn't the house be too cold for study at such a time?"

"Not if Mrs. Hemenway'd let me build up the fire for her in the living room." The boy's blue eyes fixed those of the Principal.

"Well, if you want to try it, and Mrs. Hemenway's willing for you to get the fire going early, I won't say no. But don't feel bad if you decide later it's too much."

The classes were small, ten or fifteen, and the students seemed to be friendly. The girls, though just as friendly, Calvin didn't pay much attention to right then. Some of the boys came in from local farms, having walked several miles in the early morning cold, to get there on time for the first class.

General Assembly came after the first two classes. It was held in a big upstairs room, the main body of the earlier meeting house. The faculty, two of them women, sat on the platform with Mr. Sherman, who read from the Bible. Then there was a song "America the Beautiful" this one happened to be. Calvin remembered the "templed hills" and the "waving fields of grain."

After that, Mr. Sherman gave a little talk. Though there were several other new pupils with the start of the "spring term," Calvin thought Mr. Sherman was speaking to him, for the Principal remarked in the course of his talk that a good mind is much like a good horse. "He'll do equally well on any good road." The point seemed to be that if you take a good mind and train it, you can do pretty much anything you want — an idea not unfamiliar to Calvin.

Classes ended at three. Some of the boys had to be home in time for milking. It would take those who went to Andover, or to Weston, for instance, a good hour to hike over the mountain to the little town on the West River. Rufus and Henry, and another boy named Bert — Albert Sargent — asked Calvin to go with them sliding. "Bert has an extry sled you can borrow," Rufus explained.

But Calvin didn't much want to go sliding. He wasn't much on sliding anyway, unless everything that he ought to do was already done. And he had a load of work. All these books he had accumulated as he went to classes — books and note pads he'd be filling with neat commentary as he studied.

Mrs. Hemenway came out of a downstairs room as Calvin entered the kitchen. "Afternoon classes go as well as the morning?" she asked cheerfully. "Later on you may want to put yourself up a lunch so you can get acquainted with students from the outlying villages: Proctorsville and Cavendish, Andover and Weston. Some pretty rugged farm boys in those hills. They can milk and pitch hay and plow with the best of them. Rufus learned a lot of new things in that week he spent with you."

Calvin grinned at this listing of farm chores. "P'raps I'll get to go home with one of these boys sometime and see how they handle chores down Ludlow way."

But it wasn't curiosity about differing milking methods that impelled this remark. It helped just to think about what he would be doing at home. Reluctantly he undid the strap about his books and picked out the French book. The class was a good half way through the book. He tried to study out the phonetic spelling of the strange words in the vocabulary of Lesson XI, where they were starting. They made no sense at all. He tried reading some of the story paragraph at the end of the lesson. No sense in that — just a few words which seemed to have sneaked in from English. He sat staring at the page, but the picture of his grandfather's barn intervened. Spotty, and Spotty's heifer, Hillary, so-called because he had found her on a little hill that morning now so far back. Hillary had just freshened, and she was going to be a good milker, a real good milker. Merrill generally milked her, while Calvin milked Spot, who gave a good pail full.

He began to feel funny at the pit of his stomach. Something he'd eaten? Lunch was three hours back, almost. It couldn't be that.

Not wanting to disturb Mrs. Hemenway, he put on his jacket and hat and went downstairs, keeping close to the banister so as not to make a board creak. The outside air felt good. He breathed it in longingly. But instead of its helping, it made him feel worse. He went along Pleasant Street back to the Weston road, and out that road past the little bridge his father had directed him over the day before. A deep gloom settled over him, a haze of depression. His stomach felt worse. Pretty soon they would be starting milking at Grandpa's. He wondered if his father would help Merrill, taking

Calvin's place. This idea made him feel still worse. As if to escape it, he set out along the Weston road with determined stride. The Village houses fell behind him. Big sweeps of open country, backed by woods, replaced the houses. Now and then a cluster of farm buildings. As he approached one such set of buildings, he recognized the familiar arrangement: the barnyard, and a long cattle run leading to the ample pasture, backed by woods. Just at that moment the smell of a manure pile came to his eager nostrils. City folk may not realize how like this smell can be to a fragrance. His eyes searched the area. There it was: a big, steaming pile of cow manure and straw ripening together, and the sleigh tracks out through the snow to it. He stopped to enjoy the fragrance.

Suddenly an outlandish noise assailed his ears, discordant, rhythmic, strange. He looked more closely at that muddy barnyard. There beside a corncrib stood an ungainly creature, gray against the gray barns. From pictures of the manger scene in Sunday school books they had used at home, he recognized this animal as a donkey. Long ears, body much smaller than a horse: that was just it. Wonder what they used it for. Perhaps he'd get to know this family some day, and would find out. He turned to start back, feeling guilty at the time he'd lost from study.

As he headed back, the feeling which had brought him out returned. It was a sickening, helpless feeling in the pit of his stomach. It got worse as he thought about it. It occurred to him that he could take this little bridge on the way back, the one to the Weston road, and be off for Plymouth. He'd be home by early evening. Wouldn't his father be glad to see him.

Glad? He'd be sad. He thought of the sugarhouse wood: "I've never run out on an obligation", he heard his father saying. "What I had to do, I did; and if there was a promise I'd made, I kept it, no matter what it cost me." After this little lecture, in the early morning he would take Calvin back down to Ludlow, and all the neighbors would know that John's son had run out on an obligation.

He passed that bridge without crossing it. He tried to get upstairs without being seen, but Rufus was working by the living room stove, stacking armfuls of wood beside its ample base. "Where were you?"

Rufus asked. "I thought you came home to study."

"I did. Just stepped out a minute to get some fresh air." Kind of a long "minute", he reflected. I won't let myself think about the Notch any more, leastwise I won't give in to it. "You're in my algebra class, aren't you, Henry? I might come over this evening if you'd like me to help you with your work."

* * * *

This wasn't the end of homesickness for the country boy in the big city, but further attacks were manageable. When he thought of home, he also thought of his father, and heard him saying, "If I knew I wanted a thing, I went after it and got it."

Classes were exciting. Mr. Sherman taught the class in ancient history. He had a way of bringing to life those ancient times. The bright sun of Hellas shone over the marvelous buildings on the Acropolis. After the glory that was Greece came the grandeur that was Rome; the heated debates in the Forum on issues of democrary and tyranny. The Roman legions marched again; Julius Caesar fell, victim of envious daggers, and what was to have been a benevolent dictatorship turned into a heartless despotism. But the struggle for human freedom went on. Perhaps the greatest document in that struggle to date has been the American Constitution. With a class in civil government Calvin studied this remarkable instrument of democracy, filled with increasing admiration for it the more he studied it. According to the teacher, all the strength and power of the American people, all their happiness and their prosperity, flowed from this one matchless document and its benign influence. Thus the whole course of world history led to this culminating event. The boy was filled with admiration for the great men who pondered the issues of human society and framed the rules which established American pre-eminence. It was an intoxicating thought! Bellerophon had begun his magic journey. . .

Ludlow was a friendly town. All the merchants, and as Calvin began to discover, all the lawyers knew and respected John Coolidge. Being Mr. Coolidge's son was an open sesame all the length of

Main Street. And Aunt Sarah Pollard, his mother's sister, was a haven in a storm — literally. His father had said, "If there's a bad storm on, or one coming, Calvin, your Aunt Sarah would like you should come and spend the weekend in Proctorsville. Park's 'most your age, or a little older. Dallas is about eight. If I'm not at the Hemenways' by three-thirty or soon after, then I'm not coming, and you go over to Aunt Sarah's. I want you to get to know her better anyway. She's very much like your mother."

By the time school ended in early May — so the farm boys could be ready for the season's work on the farm, and the older girls could teach at the little schools that kept during the summer for younger children — by the end of school, Calvin had begun to feel at home with classes, his school friends, and with the whole town of Ludlow. It was a good life, after all, but the summer at home was better. Given his "druthers," he'd still choose Captain over Pegasus any day.

IX

SPRINGTIME TO HARVEST

Though the Academy provided a good life, the pull of familiar scenes, of people Calvin had known all his life, led the boy to count the days to the end of that longed-for first week in May, when school would be out for the summer vacation. Vacation? For Calvin, as for most students at the Academy, it was a matter of changing one type of work, that involving books and recitations and the memorizing of many famous bits of literature, for the more accustomed work of the family farm.

The first full day back home in early May dawned as beautiful as if it were Paradise. When he stepped out on the eastern porch to smell the clean, cool air of spring, the first thing he heard was the clang of Merrill's anvil. Calvin jumped down off the porch and made his way to the little blacksmith shop. Merrill's sinewy right arm was lifted to strike a piece of glowing metal; his left hand gripped the great forcips. From the doorway Calvin watched his old friend's complete absorption in his work.

"Cutter bar broken?" the boy asked from the doorway when the blacksmith paused to stoke up his fire with the bellows.

"Calvin! Glad t'see yuh! How are you, my boy?" The man strode over to take the boy's hand in an iron grip.

"Middlin'," Cal replied. No hay-cutting yet, is there?"

"No, there ain't. But this is the liftin' rig from your father's mower. Folks with scythes are going to make remarks if'n we come up to hayin' time and then find the machine don't work. — Same's I allus mend the syrup vat in February, and the plowshares in March. You home for the summer now? I bin savin' you all my heavy work, like the rims on that dump cart out there — after you git the plowin' done."

"Good," the boy answered, knowing his friend full well. "Today I got to take Captain out for a real run. Be good for his nerves. He's all nerved up: tired of that old barn, and his coat looks kind of poor."

"Well, he's bin a wait'n fur yuh," Merrill answered as he turned back to his work.

Captain nickered joyfully from the old barnyard, extending his long face over the stone fence to greet his friend. The boy stepped over to pat him and to give him some sugar lumps from his pocket, then he turned to the old gray farmhouse where he knew he would find his grandmother.

"So you've finished the first term of your new life," his grandmother beamed at him over her spectacles. "On balance, is it as good as you felt it would be? Tell me about it."

Calvin answered the old lady's questions, then turned to leave.

"Well, it sounds as if you'd found it a good life. Glad to get home, I know, but now that you're acquainted down Ludlow way, you'll look forward to getting back in the fall. Life is good, isn't it? The start of this second phase, just as the first has been your growing up here on the farm. As you ride off with Captain on this day of full vacation your father wanted you should have, you might discuss with your four-footed friend what the *next* phase of your life should be."

"Next phase?"

"Yes, before you go back to the Academy you should choose the kind of courses you want, whether college prep or general. Latin and Greek if it's college. You may not see it all now, but you'll want to plan so's you can do a number of different things. I think your father means to talk this over with you. The more education, you know, the more choices you have. Your grandfather would be the first to admit that you can run a better farm if you have a trained, well-stocked mind."

"Is all that what Papa means by 'keeping your options open'?" Cal asked.

" 'Options'? Yes, that's another way of putting it, I guess. You and Captain talk it over. Can I give you a nice piece of mince pie to go with that apple pie Martha probably put in the lunch for you?"

The mid-morning sun of a perfect spring day was streaming down as Calvin turned Captain to the road past the blacksmith shop, past the stone school house and on up the steep grades to the Hall farmhouse at the top. Then the land started sloping down toward the Woodward Reservoir — Long Pond it had been in the old days, or Mr. Woodward's Pond.

The song sparrows were singing at their best, the bluebirds were giving that wonderful warbling call which speaks of bursting buds and herbage steaming in the sun. The purple trillium were in full bloom along the roadside, and here and there a jack-in-the-pulpit. The fiddle-heads were unfurling. Violets, blue and white and yellow, dotted color along the edges of the road where there was shade. The delicate fragrance of the small white violet mingled with the sweet smell of springing grass. It was a great time to be alive. They had come to the really steep grades now, and Captain slowed to a walk. His eager rider drank in the beauty of the scene. Every gray granite boulder he knew, every view down over the pasture land he loved. Even Grassy Pond, with its treacherous rim of quicksand seemed to invite rather than menace. He knew every foot of the familiar scene.

As Calvin reached the Hall place at the top, and was about to let Captain out on the gentle slope down toward the Reservoir — feeling a little guilty at not stopping to find Dell (Merrill told him his friend was working for the Halls), the door from the living room opened and Mrs. Hall called to Calvin: "You home for the summer, Calvin? . . . Well, good. Dell's out with Oric plowing the back lot. He'll be glad to see you."

"Good," Cal called back, with the beginning of the tactful rejoinder, "I was figgering to find him when I come back this afternoon."

"Down to the Reservoir? Don't fall in." The door closed, and Calvin was left alone with his thoughts. Why didn't Dell warm up to the idea of going away for more schooling? "I'm doing all right," Dell had answered when his friend brought up the matter. "What do I want all that Latin stuff for? Won't help me raise any better sheep, will it?"

Why didn't he agree with his chum about the sheep. Didn't he want to come back to the farm and raise sheep and fine horses like Captain? It would be back among the people he loved and in one of the best towns of the state he loved. Yet — "Keep your options open," he could hear his father saying.

The down grade was steeper now, falling off toward the Reservoir, and he reined Captain in. There was another voice speaking to him now, another thought, another idea. "No better life in the world than a farmer's" it was saying. "A farmer's life is always varied; it changes along of the seasons. First, before the snow gets too deep, there's the good hard work of cutting two years ahead the wood for sugaring and for the house. The Lord takes two years to cure that wood just right. Then the sap starts to flow 'long the middle of March. And there's fences to mend before plowing time. Then planting. Sheep-shearing, and watching the new foals running in the pasture. After that haying, and tending the crops. Then God's bounty starts to reward us for our labor: those big early Astrakhan apples and the first apple pies. Corn and beans and summer squash and greens. And the peahens' broods start feathering out, and the banties are growing up. There's corn husking bees and apple paring parties and the general harvest with crops to be put down in the root cellar, and the cider barrels to fill. Then good fat poultry to dress off, and pork to put down in brine, and we're ready for the winter with the cellar, the corncrib, and the hay mows filled, the cattle barn full of new stock — with a good lot to sell — our cash crop. Oh, it's a good life, Calvin. You couldn't do better."

Still, keep your options open. He had passed the old Jabe Morgan place and the Bishops, glad not be be hailed and made to stop and talk. He passed the Lynds' place as the road to the dam curved around the Lynds' barns. Beside the dam he dismounted and let Captain graze along the roadsides while he sat down on the edge of the dam with his lunch. It was good to look out over the water — and think.

As he retraced his course past the Lynds, the Bishops — they were still out in the big Bishop fields — he decided to take the trail on around the Reservoir past the Crandall place and down the old dirt road to the Union. Passing the Gilson place, with its remarkable ginger-bread house above Black Pond, he looked for signs of anybody living there, but it was too early. He had hardly thought of Midge since he had passed this sparkling pond the year before. But he was only thirteen then, and girls didn't mean much to him; now he was nearly fourteen and things were different. Yes, he'd be glad to see Midge Gilson. . .

X

COUNTRY SQUIRE

"So this is Sherburne Pass." It was Dell Ward speaking. In the early daylight they could see the clustered buildings of Rutland in the distance ahead of them.

"Haven't you been over the Pass before?" John Coolidge asked his son's friend.

"Yes, but I was so little; I 'most don't remember it."

"We should have taken Dell when we went to the circus early-on," Calvin remarked to his father.

"I don't think Mrs. Hall quite wanted you to go to the circus, Dell," John Coolidge observed. "She didn't act impressed when I told her we were going. Afraid of pick-pockets, perhaps."

"That wasn't it," Dell responded slowly. "Me and Oric — my brother and I had been mending fence in the west pasture. My arms got sore lifting those heavy stones. From the west pasture it was only a little farther to the Reservoir. We thought we'd catch some perch for supper."

"Any luck?" Cal asked.

"Yuh, but it didn't make no difference. Mr. Hall was mad because we didn't finish the pasture and Mrs. Hall got mad because she wanted us to work in the garden the next day."

"Still," John Coolidge observed, "if you two boys have hired out to the Halls your time is theirs."

"Anyway, the Fair's better than any old circus," Cal remarked sympathetically. "We're going to see a lot of good farm stock, cows like Spotty, only bigger, and lots of calves and yokes of oxen."

"And perhaps some peacocks like what your grandpa used to have," Cal's father added.

Even in Rutland it seemed a lot of people knew Mr. Coolidge. The boys leaned over the stock pens examining the calves and the lambs and the little pigs with a professional air, making shrewd comments to each other on the fine points of each animal. But the horses were the main attraction. Nowhere did they find any steed as beautiful as the big white bulk of Captain. Armed with generous bags of buttered pop corn, the boys sat through the races, having persuaded John Coolidge that a day at the Rutland Fair wouldn't be complete without seeing the races.

The inspiration from the Fair lasted all through the next week, involving much comparing of the Coolidge and the Hall stock with the Rutland prize winners, not infrequently to the disparagement of the latter. And the pumpkins and the Hubbard squash in the Coolidge garden were certainly better, and bigger, than what they'd seen at Rutland.

"As for me, when I grow up," Dell remarked when he stopped in on the Coolidges' at supper time the next day, "I'm going to train me a pair of oxen that will run circles around that pair at the Fair that drawed the big load of stone."

"And I'm going to raise some Arabian horses," his friend boasted. "Why, that stock that Grampa had can run twice as fast as those slow-pokes at the Fair. I'm sure going to do better with the Coolidge stock than what we saw yesterday."

"Well," his father ventured, "that's fine, and I'm sure you could. But let's not decide it all today."

* * * *

The only thing the matter with the husking bee that took place a week or so before the end of the long vacation was that Midge Gilson and her sisters had already left the house on Black Pond. Forgetting that when Midge was there during the summer he had been too shy to do more than ride by her house several times, he saw himself stepping up to Midge with a gleaming red ear of corn and claiming the kiss that was his due. The last time he rode by she had caught him. She was out in the flower garden behind the picket fence, and called out to him, "Come see my dahlias."

Calvin reined in Captain, who was accustomed to walk very deliberately past this enchanted area anyway.

The splashes of brilliant orange and red were something to marvel at, almost like his grandfather's riot of crimson and scarlet.

"And did you see this spider's gauze over here?" Midge pointed to the modest, three-petalled spiderwort with their mounds of long, grass-like leaves. "They're real old-fashioned flowers. My aunt who lives out on the Island gave us these, and this magenta variety also. Don't you think they're pretty?" She led the boy from one wonder to another. "These peonies come out when the iris are through blossoming. Look, here's one of the blue iris still in blossom. How do you like the contrast between its deep blue and this deep red dahlia?"

Calvin allowed it was real pretty, then he ventured to mention his grandfather's flower garden, not a magnificent rectangle like this, but still something to see in its wide borders along by the house. But Grandfather had a lot of farm work to do, and he couldn't spend too much time with the flowers.

"Did I hear that Captain was one of his best Arabian horses?" Midge asked. "I love horses. Would he let me pat him?"

Calvin assured Midge that Captain was gentle as a lamb.

Everybody who had a good stand of field corn managed to set up a husking bee during the Sunday afternoons of autumn, till it got too cold for this to be fun any more. Everybody knew that a husking bee was work, too, but the occasion was so garnished with hilarity and rewarded further by generous slices of fruit cake and new cider that the work was no work at all. The hilarity came from the discovery of a red ear. The "bee" usually took place on the main floor of a barn. The walls or the bulging hay mows along the sides of this main floor where the hay wagons were drawn in and unloaded — the walls were concealed by huge dry corn stalks, some from which the ears had not been pulled. But the main dish was the bushel baskets full of ears to be husked. These ran all along the sides of the main floor. A farmer always planted a certain percentage — not a large one — of red flint corn. Anyone finding such a red ear was privileged to take the ear to whatever pretty girl he fancied and claim a kiss. It worked the same way for girls, too, when they found red ears — sort of like a Sadie Hawkins dance.

The Coolidge "bee" was set for the last Sunday afternoon before the Academy fall term began. It took place in the capacious barn of the Coolidge farm, Grandpa Galusha Coolidge's barn. When the baskets were all emptied of corn ears and the standing dry stalks had been searched for extra ears, the large corn crib beside the barn would be full, and the poultry and the horses would enjoy the contents all winter. Grandma Coolidge, with her son, John Coolidge, kept up the tradition. It was never hard to get folks to come to the Coolidge bee: the Coolidge fruit cake, washed down with ample portions of Coolidge sweet cider, was famous.

Some thirty people turned up for the occasion, including a goodly number from the Union — Unionville on the old maps — and from Frog City and beyond. The Blanchards were there, and the Wards; the Pinneys came from Pinney Hollow and the McWains from down beyond Frog City. The Moors were out in force, several families of them; several branches of the Coolidge clan were represented. It was more the young folks than the older group. After much banter and home-spun jokes, the group settled down to the matter in hand, which was ears of corn. The first whoop marking the husking of a red ear came from somebody down Frog City way. He jumped up and strode along the double line to hold out the trophy to the girl of his choice. Nothing loath, she jumped up and grasped the ear at the same time he grasped her. The sidelines cheered.

The group went back to work. But every so often there would be a whoop or a squeal of delight, and somebody would jump up to claim his (or her) prize.

Calvin had often dreamt of what girl of those present he would choose when and if the choice came to him. When it did, he was

overwhelmed with bashfulness. With face as red, almost, as the ear of corn he held, he made his way over to Stella McWain, two years older and the friend of sister Abbie: he knew her well. She stood up, expectantly. For a moment Calvin hesitated. Was the boy going to lose his nerve? Stella was equal to the emergency. "Well, you want a kiss, don't you? Come on then." The whole group cheered when the Coolidge son and heir finally claimed his reward.

By milking time the piles were gone; the gleaming ears had been taken out to the corn crib and everybody sat down again to enjoy the Coolidge refreshments.

The last day of summer vacation was a drowsy day in early October; Calvin thought of the poem of Celia Thaxter's he had learned in "literature class,"

"When loud the bumble bee makes haste,
Belated, thriftless vagrant;
And on the ground red apples lie,
And lanes with grapes are fragrant."

The red apples were part of it, he reflected, and the "bright, blue weather."

He gazed off at the serrated line of mountains to the east, blue in the autumn haze. But the lanes fragrant with grapes had somehow missed the area. Still, there were Baldwins and Tinmouth and Sheep Nose and Russets, the last not much on looks but mellow and spicy at the end of winter. Then in the cellar were those two barrels of Northern Spies. He remembered them with pleasure, for he had had a special part in picking them. The trees were so high that his father's ladder failed to reach the topmost branches, and Cal had had to shinny up the soaring limbs and pick the apples, clinging precariously perched along a branch. He tossed the fruit down one at a time to his father, who set them in the basket carefully so no bruise, unnoted now, could start the rot later on. Those two barrels were stored carefully in a cool dark corner of the cellar. They'd be just right to start bringing out after the Christmas holidays, along with the Sickel pears. In his mind he went over the list of the root crops stored in the dark of the cellar: a big bin of gleaming potatoes; it was always fun to dig those Green Mountain potatoes, trying to guess with each hill just how many gold nuggets he'd find.

There were beets, too, winter beets, big ones, but sweet and juicy when the red slices were dripping with butter. Of carrots there were almost too many. Certainly he felt that way when his aching shoulders had carried baskets and buckets of them, carefully packed in sand, down the treacherous stone steps of the hatchway. Turnips, too — some would go to Captain during the winter — and some parsnips, though the main part of the crop was left in the ground. "Much better if they freeze," Grandpa had always remarked. There were cabbage heads, too, enough to last all winter; and some of those new brussels sprouts.

The punkins and the big hubbard squash were stored in the attic, along with the braids of onions, and the dried slices of apples for winter pies. Along with the apples, the rows and rows of canned peas and beans and other goodies in mason jars, the jellies and the apple butter, were what Grandpa meant by "riches." Altogether, with the fat roasting fowl and the pork and mutton, they could live like kings all through the time of snows. Yes, it was certainly a good life, and fun, most of it, at any rate, and varied enough with the seasons to miss being monotonous. Riding Captain around the farm, he felt like a country squire counting his ample stores.

Captain, or Pegasus? Perhaps at the end of the next school year at the Academy, he could better decide this issue.

XI

PEGASUS TAKES OFF

Calvin was quickly caught up in the two attractions at Black River Academy: old friends, and classes which under the dedicated skills of teachers who themselves loved learning, communicated its excitements to eager youngsters. Settling in now to choices which his preliminary term had enabled him to assess more accurately, he continued French and started Latin. "You want to be able to write clearly and effectively, don't you?" Mr. Kendall looked over the tops of his steel-rimmed glasses at the boy, seated timidly across from the great man. "Of course you want to be able to write well, and to speak easily in the Speaking Classes on Friday afternoons. Let me tell you something: I have never known a man to be able to write clearly and precisely without a background of Latin. Latin gives you a feeling for sentence structure, and a precision in the use of words. These are impossible without Latin." Mr. Kendall shot a piercing glance at the boy. "Did you ever try to read the stuff sent in for the weekly newspapers, stuff written by people with practically no education? They do the best they can, of course, but try to figure out what they want to say. The ideas get lost in a welter of words and dubious grammar."

Of course Calvin started Latin. How could he do otherwise?

The next year, Calvin's sophomore year, there was a new principal, George Sherman, who persuaded the boy to start Greek. This was in addition to more Latin, more French, along with algebra and civics, or "civil government." Somehow, American literature, some rhetoric and the Friday afternoon "speaking" got squeezed in too.

Greek was almost the straw that broke the camel's back. Besides the strange alphabet to master, the Greek characters, there were not two voices, but three: an active, a middle, and a passive. And in Homeric Greek there was a third number, in between the singular and the plural: the dual, not much used, but it added to the load. Calvin was not by nature a student who stood at the top of his class; the dogged persistence which gained the boy a creditable standing almost gave out. Calvin realized, in time, that once you let a Greek lesson slip, you were *lost*. With his usual methodical thoroughness, he went back over previous lessons and got them all into his head by dint of much writing out of declensions and conjugations, paradigms and phonetic changes. But it was work, sheer, grubby, sweaty work, with the reward, in the "March of the Ten Thousand" and in Homer's sonorous periods, still a year or two away. In the evenings, by the light of the oil lamp, he dozed over his Greek grammar till he heard his father's voice say, "I never ran out on a duty." Then he would get up, take a turn around the room, and settle back to his struggle with the Hellenic idiom.

Several students in his class gradually became his companions. Rufus Hemenway, of course, in whose house he roomed the first year, and Henry Brown. Then Bert Sargent, a tall, happy-go-lucky youngster, full of fun and the sap of life. Roy Bryant, also, from the class below him, was part of the "gang," if a loner could be said to share in a gang. Together they fished in the clear waters of Black River, or raided the orchards up the Weston road, or — as happened more than once — launched a pat of butter, on the end of a knife, sling-shot style, to lodge on a beam over the teacher's desk. When the room heated up after the first class, the butter lump melted enough to fall in a shapeless splat on books or papers gracing the preceptorial desk. The results were sometimes too devastating to be risked more than once in a year. The unsuspected culprits felt bound together by the spicy tang of danger. It was a good feeling, one fairly new to Calvin.

The Academy was not a thing apart. There was no town and gown hostility; Ludlow had, after all, started the Academy, pledging the funds and the labor to put up the original building if the projected school would locate in the town. Old-timers among the merchants spoke with pride of how they had helped build that first structure. This was in 1835, over fifty years ago. When the building burned down a decade later, the town approved the arrangement by which the Baptists, prime movers in starting the school, sheltered the academic activities in the straitened, but adequate, confines of the "Meeting House" atop the next knoll.

"Yup, we're mighty proud of the old Academy," one merchant told Calvin. "My wife and I both graduated from the Academy, back in the fifties, same as your father and mother did. And when they had the big fiftieth anniversary celebration year before last, folks who'd studied at the Academy came from all over the country. Twenty-six states represented, and more'n half of Ludlow and Cavendish, and Proctorsville. Why, folks that grew up together at the Academy practically cried when they met at that reunion. We all love the Academy."

Sometime, along in Calvin's junior year, the student came to life. What he had done earlier with dogged determination and as a duty, he began to perform now with deep interest and new understanding. He started to realize how the torch of civilization, first lighted in the Euphrates valley and along the Nile, carried by new migrations to the Tagus at Athens and the Tiber in Rome, swept on to the banks of the Thames, the Seine and the Potomac, thence on to the mighty Mississippi and the Rio Grande and the Columbia. It was a startling progression when you saw it all together. And our own feeling for democracy, begun so long ago in Greece, refined in Rome, carried on into the struggle with the English kings, reached full flower in the American Constitution and the Bill of Rights. Bellerophon was taking off!

The realization of what the fine old Academy stood for may have been furthered by the occasional visits of a distinguished alumnus among them, Captain Henry Atherton of Nashua, who had been the principal speaker for the School at its Fiftieth Anniversary. More than once Captain Atherton had stood at the rostrum in the assembly room of the old Meeting House and addressed the student body, sharing his appreciation for his beloved Alma Mater.

"Boys and girls, I don't come here this morning like some old moss-back, to tell you to 'study hard and get good marks'. I come here to tell you that I know as a student here myself some of the trials you have to suffer. The algebra that never comes out right; the Greek which is just plain incomprehensible; that poem of which I forgot the second line at 'Speaking'. But with all the pain and struggle each night as you try to get your lessons, there's something else I remember: the sheer joy of learning, the satisfaction of obstacles overcome, the delight in dark ignorance dispelled by the light of understanding, the dawn of comprehension of how all knowledge fits together.

"And now I realize as I only dimly saw when I was a student here — I realize the devotion of your teachers. They didn't come here for money. If that had been their motivation they would have gone elsewhere. They came here because of the sheer love of learning, and their desire to share its pleasures with youth. It's a great institution, my friends, this old Academy, and I love it. I would like to leave for the student body to reflect on, a little prayer for the Academy, addressed to you, my Alma Mater. Here it is; I'll write it out on the blackboard, so those who haven't fully mastered the Latin idiom can reach for it and discover, I hope, the full meaning of what I'm writing:

Vives et crescas; floreasque in aeterno, saecula saeculorum." But the fine old Academy did not "live and grow forever." It closed its doors in 1924 and the Ludlow high school took over.

Unlike some schools, the Academy took a lively interest in politics, both local and national. The contest between Grover Cleveland and Benjamin Harrison in 1888 became a focus for this political ardor. Most of the town and therefore most of the student body, so closely linked to the town, were staunch Republicans. They were determined to turn out the incumbent, Grover Cleveland, and seat their champion, the Republican Harrison. It was a hot contest, and when finally Harrison had won, the celebration that followed was partly a release of tension. For two nights along the main street there were parades of townsfolk and students, with much singing, shouting, and the boom of drums, the blare of trumpets. At a big bonfire that first night, the unhappy Mr. Cleveland was burned in effigy. The exultation at this demise of a Democrat exceeded all bounds.

"Know what we ought to do?" Calvin asked as he stood with several friends watching the holocaust.

"What?" Bert Sargent asked. "Name it and we'll do it. Anything that's more fun than this I want to know about."

"Well," Calvin drawled. "Rufus, you know that donkey your cousins have out on the Weston road? Name's Jenny, isn't it? She hangs around that corncrib."

"Yeah," Rufus said, studying his friend's face as it was revealed in the firelight.

"Think we could borrow her tomorrow night?"

"To put in the parade?" Bert asked. "Great idea, eh Rufe? Sign on it, something about 'Too bad, Democrats. We weep for you'?"

"No," Calvin broke in. "Not in the parade. *After* the parade, when the town's gone to bed, we could get her up to old Dickinson's classroom. He's been mighty quiet, recently, and I think he's a Democrat."

"He's no Democrat," Henry Brown spoke up. "He's a good fellow; I like him."

"Well, if he didn't teach Greek I could get more het up about him," Calvin answered, "but no matter. We can get her up there, the four of us; I know we can. And Bert's sign's a fine idea. Only let's have it say, 'Bray for us poor Democrats.'"

"Hey, that's great," Rufus said, his voice sinking to a conspiratorial whisper. "I'll ask the Pollards tomorrow to see can we have her."

"No," Calvin spoke emphatically. "Your folks might say you couldn't. That would spoil the whole plan. If you want to do something, want it real bad, do it first and take the consequences. But nobody's going to know who took the donkey, and the Academy can take her back."

Bert Sargent had become thoughtful. "How well do you know

Jenny, Rufe? She likely to get ornery? They say most donkeys are ornery."

"She like carrots?" Cal asked quickly. "You could borrow a few from your mother's cellar."

"Let's get enough fellows to be sure Jenny goes up those stairs," Bert suggested.

"No," Cal said once more. "Four is all we need. The more fellows the more chance of somebody blabbing, especially if they make a real search at school to find who did it."

Rufus and Henry, it was agreed, would hike out the Weston road to escort Jenny in. Bert and Calvin would meet them at the Academy door, which was never locked. By the time Rufus and Henry showed up with their long-eared friend, the whole town was quiet. The two boys at the Academy door had watched the lights go out, one by one, till the whole area was dark.

Silently the two watchmen held the big door open. Rufus and Henry stepped into the silent hall.

"You got your carrots?" Cal asked Rufus.

"'Nuf for two donkeys," the boy replied, taking a long carrot out of his coat pocket.

"Bert and I'll mind the rear. Speak to Jenny kind of gentle, and show her the carrot."

Poor Jenny's trust in Rufus got her up the first few steps. Then the enticement of the carrot helped. Fortunately it was a short flight of steps, for part way up the stairs Calvin, wise in the ways of animals, felt Jenny's flank muscles tighten. The sharp slap he gave her on the rear-end surprised the animal into going forward a few more steps, and then the trip was over.

"You know what I forgot?" Rufus whispered. "I was going to find a piece of cardboard from a suit box or something so we could write that sign you suggested."

"Oh, we'll get along," Calvin retorted. "Better on the blackboard anyway, over to one side of where Dickinson sits. You got a good hand, Henry. Why don't you write it? Only make it block letters, so the handwriting won't give you away."

Laboriously, while the rest watched, Henry chalked out, by the

light of the moon, the legend: "Bray for us poor Democrats."

"Now remember," Cal cautioned as the guilty foursome sneaked down the creaking stairs, "Remember, mum's the word. And don't you tell Suzie Pollard about it, Bert. A joke's a lot better if they can't figure out who did it."

The mystification was complete. The janitor didn't hear Jenny on the floor above till many of the students had arrived. Then he led the placid animal back down the stairs, speaking to her encouragingly with each step. The students were so taken aback that they watched this amazing spectacle in silence, thus keeping Jenny from getting alarmed. The legend on the far blackboard was discovered with the first class, and everyone had a good laugh all over again.

Fortunately George Sherman knew teen-agers well enough not to use the device of asking the perpetrators of this prank to own up, a development which Calvin had feared. The boys were the Principal's loyal supporters ever after.

A week later, a bushel of choice Northern Spies awaited the janitor when he came in to build the fires. The sign on it read — in block letters — "For a good sport." The janitor, being scrupulously honest, told George Sherman about the apples and wondered if they were meant for the Principal.

"No, John, it's you they meant. I didn't have that mess to clean up in Dickinson's room."

Years later Calvin wrote of this and similar episodes: "About as far as I deem it prudent to discuss my own connection with these escapades is to record that I was never convicted of any of them and so must be presumed innocent."

* * *

The demands of serious study in this junior year left little time for pranks. The nine members of the class of 1890 were beginning to think about the future. The earlier question in Calvin's mind, that of whether to follow his grandfather Coolidge and take over the farm or to seek further fields was about settled in favor of the latter. Principal Sherman and Belle Chellis, Preceptress, had not a little to do with this decision.

George Sherman was impressed with the boy's come-back in Greek. "For a while there, we thought you were lost," George Sherman confessed when Calvin sought the man out for some light on his future. "But the way you gained ground again, when you were at last convinced you had to put forth an almost heroic effort to catch up. This convinces me that you can handle anything at college."

"But I don't seem ever to make the top in the class," Cal objected.

"Maybe not, and maybe you will yet. But you've got what it takes, besides a good, well-ordered mind: that's persistence. You never give up. Once started on something you'll see it through, no matter what it may cost in effort. Oh, it would be a shame for you not to go to college, Calvin, since your father can afford to send you."

During this time Calvin had moved from the Hemenway house to the Pinneys', with a boy named Coburn as his roommate. Thence, in 1888, Calvin moved on to his Aunt Sarah's in Proctorsville, where there were two Pollard boys, Dallas, five years younger than Calvin, and Park, several years older. It was then that Calvin wrote his father to give his sister Abbie the advantage Calvin had had, of a preliminary term at the Academy to get her bearings. Aunt Sarah gave Calvin, and later Abbie as well, something of the warm mothering the Coolidge children had so tragically lost three years before.

When Abbie came to join Calvin she impressed everyone not only with her blond beauty — she had her mother's auburn hair and good looks — but with her practical good sense, her intelligence, and her charm. In bad weather the pair took the train from Rutland, which reached Ludlow in the late afternoon, and got off at Proctorsville, all of three miles away. A ride on the steam cars was always a thrill to the two children from the deep country.

Belle Chellis, the assistant principal, spoke to Calvin as she saw him passing her door. "This a study period for you, Calvin?" she asked.

The boy nodded.

"I thought it was, and I'd like to take a little piece of it if I may, to talk with you. First to tell you something I guess you know: we all love your sister Abbie. She's so modest and so intelligent."

"She's like my mother," Calvin replied, with the suggestion still of a quaver in his voice.

"I'm sure she is, and your mother would be proud of both of you. You've grown up so much this year, Calvin. A young man now. I hear you plan to go to college when you graduate next year? — Good. Where will you go?"

"I, I hadn't thought that far yet, Miss Chellis."

"Well, I suggest you think about Amherst. A country location, an outstanding faculty. Any idea of what you want to be?"

"I'd thought some of a lawyer. My father says that with a background of the law you can go in a number of directions."

"A fine idea. Almost anyone in government, for instance, can use some legal training. It's a good background for business, too. Calvin, I think you've got it in you to go far if you want to. One step at a time, you know. And that determination we all see in you . . . Thank you for stopping in. I shouldn't take any more of your time."

In early March of Calvin's senior year John Wilder, his mother's sister's husband, appeared one afternoon at Aunt Sarah's. Calvin greeted the young man apprehensively.

"What's wrong, John," Calvin asked.

"It's Abbie. What we thought was just a stomach upset when you left for school Sunday afternoon is something worse. The doctors don't know what it is, but your father wants you should come home."

"Is Abbie going to — going to —?" Calvin asked, unable to say the fatal word after the tragedy of his mother's death and before that, his beloved grandfather.

"We hope not, but you'll be away a few days. Your Aunt Sarah will get word to the school."

It was a gloomy, silent trip back to Plymouth, and a sad, silent household, striken by a sense of impending calamity. His father shook hands silently. "Abbie wants to see you," he said huskily. "She's been asking for you. The Doctor's given her some powders to help the pain, so she may not know you at first."

Abbie lay on her back, her blue eyes staring straight ahead.

Calvin stood looking down at her, unbelieving.

Suddenly she seemed to recognize him. She turned her head

slightly toward her brother, managed a wan smile, and brought her hand out from under the covers.

Calvin grasped it, too full of the shock of what he saw to risk words.

"So glad you came," she whispered. "Stay here — close."

That night she slipped away.

It was hard to return to the Academy and take up the life Calvin had grown to love. He missed his sister particularly on the long walks home to Proctorsville. Everyone at the Academy felt his loss. In the silent grip of friendly hands and the friendly eyes that looked into his he saw the depth of people's understanding of this new bereavement. After all, Abbie was not quite fifteen, full of bright promise. And in this close-knit family there was little of the usual sibling rivalry. Some of the boy's love for his mother had come to be bestowed on her daughter, so like the mother.

The days slipped by. Calvin forced himself to give full attention to his studies. Graduation was only two months away, and Calvin was to have a part in the ceremonies: he was to give an oration on the subject of "Oratory in History," the effect of the spoken word in determining human action. Much of what he had learned about life went into that speech, the first he had ever had to deliver before a public audience. Not only what he had learned about living, but what he had forced himself to in the weekly "Speaking" stood the shy boy in good stead on this important occasion.

And he realized why these graduation ceremonies were called "Commencement." The Reverend Evan Thomas, giving the baccalaureate sermon, spoke to a new maturity in Calvin when he remarked:

"Man . . . has within himself the power of choosing and pursuing his own ways, . . . of acting as duty directs, though he is often unconscious of the fact. When man is true to himself, within certain limits, he is not the creature of circumstance but the master of circumstances."

Calvin had proved this already; now he would commence to apply it consciously — and with determination.

XII

FORMULA FOR GREATNESS

The spring of 1891, which should have seen Calvin Coolidge finishing his first year at Amherst, was, instead, a doubtful interim. The young graduate of the Academy, well prepared by the learning he had achieved at Ludlow, was nevertheless defeated by another difficulty. When he took the train down to Amherst he still had entrance exams to pass. On the train he developed a heavy cold, which went on into the start of pneumonia. He failed his exams, came back home knowing he had, and was sick for two months. It must have been a great disappointment. He helped paint the interior of the store his father still owned. After a few weeks in the late winter at his beloved Black River Academy, he spent the spring term at St. Johnsbury Academy, where Dr. Putney, widely known as a scholar and a strict disciplinarian, put the young student through his paces, was impressed by his determination, and readily gave him a certificate which entitled him to enter Amherst without further examination.

It was during that spring of 1891 that the news of a coming dedication of the Bennington Battle Monument began to circulate through Vermont. "Calvin," John Coolidge said when he saw his son, "I think we should go to that dedication. You may never see — I know *I* shall never see — a more impressive assemblage than this will be. Folks — important people — from all over the country are coming. President Harrison will be there. They've been getting ready for it for three years; well, much more than that. It's going to be on the nineteenth of August."

"Why not have it on the sixteenth, Battle of Bennington Day?"

His father chuckled: "Vermont thrift. The nineteenth marks the date of Vermont's entering the Union. Kills two birds with one stone. This is the centennial year. Two big events to celebrate. Shall we go?"

Cal nodded. "Sounds all right to me."

The two set out on the nineteenth before daybreak, to catch the special train on the Bennington and Rutland Railroad, scheduled to arrive before the start of the big parade. Every detail had been carefully planned. The cooperation of the railroads had been enlisted, beginning with the Bennington and Rutland, the Central Vermont, the Fitchburg, the Connecticut River, the Boston and Maine, and a number of shorter lines. Printed programs of the day had been handed out on the train. These the Coolidges studied as the train clattered along. Their own planning for the day could not have exceeded the attention to detail shown by the many committees working to produce a program to go off without a hitch. When the steam cars from Rutland rolled into the Bennington station — trains were unloading on a tight schedule — John Coolidge and his son joined the throng that was pouring out of the station. Outside all was action, color, noise. People, in greater numbers than even the Rutland Fair had mustered, made a dense crowd surging toward what would be the line of march of the grand procession. Everything was wrapped in gay colored bunting, the national colors predominating. Noise, such as only a vast crowd can produce, was everywhere.

"It's half past nine," Calvin shouted in his father's ear as they strode along. "We may not be able to make it to the reviewing stand in time."

"This mob won't let us get on any faster," the elder Coolidge replied to his son's warning about the time. "But these parades never start on time."

The gigantic procession did! This enormous column, consisting of nearly a hundred different marching delegations from civic and military organizations, dozens of special carriages seating dignitaries from all over the country, boasting more than a dozen bands, mounted calvary, G.A.R. groups, etc. — this whole procession, according to the Chief Marshall's report to Governor Carroll Page, Chairman of the Committee in charge of the parade, "moved from the grounds of the Soldiers' Home *promptly* at 10 o'clock A.M." The platoon of mounted officers, warning everyone off the course of the parade, caught the Coolidges at the Triumphal Arch, not a bad place from which to view the action.

This amazing structure, a massive construction of wood, covered by canvas painted to simulate the rough stone and finished seams of the Monument itself, was seventy-five feet long, about eighteen feet wide, and fully sixty feet high. So fully was the design of a stone structure imitated that a number of people commented on the "excellent stone cutting," and the time it must have taken to construct. Others were seen to tap it with their canes to be convinced of the material.

But the most memorable feature of this structure was the group of over 175 girls and children from the public schools, dressed in white, with their hair falling loose around their shoulders. When this fascinating group sang patriotic songs and hymns, they "looked like little angels, every one of them," as one woman was heard to remark to her escort.

The only delay in the line of march had been the crowd that swarmed around the victoria, drawn by four white horses, in which sat President Harrison, Governor Carroll Page, and William Seward Webb, the Governor's aide. When this special carriage reached the Arch, the President arose and stood with uncovered head before thirteen young women ranged on the balcony below the children, representing the original Colonies. The Goddess of Liberty, bearing her torch, arose to acknowledge the President's action, and the whole vast concourse, the children's voices leading, burst into the song, "America." This was taken up by the crowds filling the streets, the housetops, the windows of buildings, till the mighty anthem rose in a pitch of patriotic fervor to bring tears to one's eyes. As the President sat down again, the victoria passed under the Arch, and the children above threw armfuls of roses down on him and on the carriage. It was a moment rare in history.

Reaching the reviewing stand at Monument Park, the President was escorted to his place of honor, surrounded by state and national dignitaries. Four guns fired in rapid succession with perfect timing, gave the twenty-one gun Presidential salute. The sight from the grandstand, as the long column wound up the hill, was the "finest and most imposing spectacle of its sort ever seen in this state."

Calvin and his father, by dint of determined effort, managed to get near enough to the reviewing stand to catch most of the words of the President's speech. Benjamin Harrison was a home-spun type, born fifty-seven years before this event, on an Ohio farm, whence he went to a log cabin school, became a lawyer by apprenticing to a law firm, moved to Indiana, was elected to the U.S. Senate and finally, by determined effort and great throroughness in detail, became our twenty-third president. He was a reserved man, often considered cold and aloof; but no one gathered around him a more devoted and loyal group of friends. He was not a tall man, but broad shouldered and well-built. Kindly eyes looked out above a full beard, and his manner of speaking was simple and direct.

Having followed the silver-tongued orator, the Honorable Edward S. Phelps of Burlington, writer and diplomat, the President was at something of a disadvantage, which he noted immediately by saying, "There are several obvious reasons why I should not attempt to speak to you at this time. This great audience is so uncomfortably situated that a further prolongation of these exercises cannot be desirable; but the stronger one is that you have just listened, with rapt attention, to a most scholarly and interesting review of those historical incidents which have suggested this assemblage . . ." The President went on to note that his talk had had to be entirely extemporaneous; briefly and graciously he brought the greetings of the other states to Vermont, and noted the properly high esteem with which they regarded the Fourteenth State.

Some 3500 of this vast audience gathered under two great canvas awnings for a formal "collation," starting about mid-afternoon. This included greetings from various states represented by their governors, and by a more formal speech from the President, who apologized for his "delapidated voice," which, he remarked, kept him from doing justice to the occasion. Though everyone had been cautioned to keep completely still, it was hard to hear the President, who was obviously making an heroic effort to speak at all.

On the way back to Rutland, Calvin, much too excited by the events of the day to sleep, sat looking at the flaring oil lamps which swayed with the lurch of the train. His father also sat in silence, reviewing in his own mind the impressive galaxy of orators to whom he had listened. "What did you think of when you got to shake hands with the President after the banquet, Calvin?"

The young man smiled. "I thought from the grip he gave me he must have handled an ax a good deal. So I gave him my strongest grip too. *I've* had an ax in my hands more than once."

His father smiled. "Yes, I guess you have. The President said something to you. What was it?"

"Oh, when I gave him my grip he just said, 'A real Vermonter, I can feel that. Glad to meet you, young man.'"

"What did you answer?"

"I — I couldn't think of anything to say," Calvin confessed.

"Well, he wasn't expecting you to, I'm sure, with all that line waiting to shake his hand. What did you think?

"Mostly of what a great man he is. What must it be like to represent the whole United States, this whole great nation, and to bear the responsibility of it all on his shoulders. What a burden. I can hardly think what it must be like."

John Coolidge chuckled. "One of my biggest moments was when I first went to the Assembly as Representative Coolidge from Plymouth and shook the hand of the Governor. He greeted me as if he'd known me as a long-time friend. Perhaps sometime you'll get to do that — or even get to Washington — who knows — and as Representative Coolidge, or Senator Coolidge, be able to shake the hand of the then president. Don't shake your head. Stranger things than that have happened. It depends on setting your sights and then persevering."

"Just as you and Grandma Coolidge have always said," Calvin

grinned.

They were silent a while. The steam cars lurched on through the night.

Then John Coolidge, following up his son's earlier remark, observed: "The responsibility you speak of, it must be something to keep you awake nights. Harrison's not a great speaker, but his personality comes through as honest, conscientious, and concerned. I can see how he gets the loyalty he does. He did pretty well in his talk at the Monument. His duties hadn't given him any time to think out a speech, but the man came through for what he is: genuine, thorough, able."

"Yeah. I was interested too because it was something he hadn't prepared. Like the speeches they used to spring on us on Speech Days. Good practice for something like this. The one that interested me most was General Howard, the man who'd lost his right arm in the war."

"Oh, the man who stood in for the Governor of New York, who didn't show up?"

"Yes, the General said he'd been asked to speak for New York just a minute or so before he had to get up. He did pretty well to get over the history of how New York tried to grab the properties in the New Hampshire Grants and how feelings had changed in this century so that New York is one of our good neighbors."

"Yes, I felt that way, too. General Howard's not only an able man, he's a truly good man: the 'praying general' they used to call him. What speech stands out among all you heard as the most memorable, the most stirring?"

"No question: it was Mr. Phelps."

"Why?"

"Well, he made me see history as I'd never viewed it before. Wish they'd have that speech printed and put in all the history books for Vermont children. I didn't realize, somehow, though I'd read about it, that this one battle probably thwarted General Burgoyne's plan for joining up with the British at Albany and New York and cutting off New England from the rest of the Colonies. Once we were cut off, they could chew us up at their leisure. And I never realized that

General Stark was so independent. He'd responded faster than anybody could imagine, when we called on New Hampshire for help. He ignored the order from the Colonies to abandon this expedition and lead his men to join Schuyler at Albany. He had no supplies, no cannon, only two moulds for making bullets, and he had to find his way through wilderness. Then he got across the Grants faster than anybody else ever could, organized the defense of Bennington, and on the sixteenth he *had* to attack, because he had no supplies to fall back on. With a mostly untrained, undisciplined force of young settlers he attacked the entrenched Hessians and the professional British soldiers and outgeneraled them all. How could he win in such circumstances? But as Phelps says — how was it he put it? — 'He lacked everything but men, and his men lacked everything but hardihood, and indomitable resolution.' Then he said of these men that 'they were fighting for all they had on earth . . . They could not go home defeated, for they would have no homes to go to.' When you see it that way, you can understand why those men could storm the breastworks of the Hessians and drive them out."

The boy's eyes glistened as his father had never seen them before.

"Makes us see how precious our freedom is," the older man commented. "I hope we never have to fight for it again, because I don't believe there was ever a dispute that couldn't be settled by understanding, but this was a bad one. It was sheer grit and determination that won out, as it generally does."

EPILOG

The story of Calvin Coolidge's boyhood and his subsequent career is one of the most inspiring bits of Americana we have. The man was no genius, nor did he have any very special talents, except, as political friends later remarked, "an uncanny sense of timing" as to when the right moment might be to launch some course of political action.

This sense of timing may have resulted because he was truly a man of the people, and could therefore feel how they would feel, react as they would react. The descendants of Stella McWain remarked that Calvin as a boy listened eagerly to adult conversations, never seeming to tire of them.

What is so inspiring about Coolidge's life is the demonstration it gives of what single-minded determination, persistence, can do for one, given some native intelligence to start with.

Years later Calvin wrote out his "Formula for Success:"

"Nothing in this world can take the place of persistence. Talent will not; nothing in this world is more common than unsuccessful men of talent. Genius will not; unsuccessful genius is almost a proverb. Education will not; the world is full of educated derelicts. Persistence and determination alone are omnipotent."

As the older man and the young man of nineteen pondered these imponderables while the coaches rattled on through the darkness toward Rutland that memorable evening of August 19, 1891, they could not know the remarkable series of steps by which the younger man mounted, one at a time, the ladder to great achievement.

It started in Northampton, Massachusetts, where, having been graduated from Amherst in 1895, young Coolidge began reading law in September of that year with a local law firm. In 1897 he was admitted to the bar and later became a member of the Republican City Committee for Ward 2. In December of 1898 he was elected a city councilman from Ward 2. The City Council elected him City Solicitor in 1900. In 1903 he was appointed Clerk of Courts of Hampshire County. In 1904 he was made Chairman of the Republican City Committee for Northhampton.

In 1905 he married Grace Goodhue of Burlington, Vermont. She became his faithful partner in all his subsequent achievements. In 1906 young Coolidge was elected Representative to the Massachusetts General Court. In December 1909 he was elected Mayor of Northhampton, beginning a continuous course of public service to March 4, 1929. He was elected a State Senator in 1911. His colleagues in the Senate elected him President of the Senate of Massachusetts in 1913. He became Lieutenant Governor of Massachusetts in 1915. In 1918 he was elected Governor of Massachusetts. The Boston Police Strike in 1919 brought him national acclaim when he stated to the president of the American Federation of Labor, "There is no right to strike against the Public Safety by anybody, anywhere, any time." On June 12, 1920, he was nominated for Vice-President by the Republican National Convention meeting in Chicago. On November 4th of that year he was elected Vice-President. In the early hours of August 3rd, 1923, at President Harding's death, he became President of the United States.

In 1924, by a landslide vote, he was elected President of the United States.

"Persistence and determination alone are onmipotent."